A F*CKERY OF SONGS & SHADOWS

A.J. BRAUN

CONTENTS

CONTENTS

1

─────────

WELCOME TO COURTCHELLA

I MUST'VE BEEN HUNGOVER, exhausted, or nursing a headache from my dragon, Benny, singing all day, because why in the literal fuck would I *ever* agree to—

"Welcome to Courtchella: Beneath the Bluffs! We're beyond excited to have a dragon and their rider as security personnel for the most attended musical festival of the year." The coordinator smiled unnervingly wide.

I couldn't decide if I wanted to hurl my axe into a rock or at Benny who chose this damn bounty hunting job.

The ocean lapped against the beach beneath us as we stood on the grassy cliff overlooking the venue. Benny's golden wings glinted in the sun as he stretched them, their span as wide as a ship is long. Endless Courtchella attendants lined the rocky cliffside, all of them laughing, drinking, and screaming with one another while an attendant reviewed their entries and stamped some kind of rune on their foreheads.

Oh, I'm so excited for this, Rhema! Hundreds of years living on the winds and I've never been able to get into Courtchella. Can you believe this is actually happening? Benny said into my mental bridge.

No, I really can't, I groaned, pushing my thought into his mind.

Rhema, Rhema, Rhema, you cranky muscle woman, you, Benny tsked. **I think you'll enjoy being down in those caverns more than you think.**

You're right, Benny. I'd so much rather be stuck underground surrounded by drunk and sweaty fanatics than be anywhere else.

Did you forget to have your snacks before we got here?

I'd forgotten, but that didn't matter, so I ignored his unimportant question. *Are you sure you're going to be alright in a cave for an entire night?*

Oh, don't worry about me. I used to hang out with a group of dragons who were avid spelunkers. He looked off into the distance with a wistful smile. **Those were the days.**

How do dragons go spelunking—? You know what, I don't want to know. Let's just get this job over with so we can collect the bounty.

Come on, I know you're just as excited as me to see Morally Gone.

I turned to him. *You know we're assigned to kill them, right?*

I mean, eventually we will—

Benny, we're not here to fangirl over an immortal bardic boy band who are brainwashing women with the Diadem of Ancient Darkness and Devoted Yearning.

You mean the DADDY.

If you call it that one more time, I'm not doing this job.

Rhema! Benny whined. **Look, I know we're going to kill them and I've made my peace with that, but that doesn't mean we can't enjoy a song or two first! Once we slay them before midnight, then diadem's powers will release the dozen or so women they were able to enchant tonight. It would be such a waste to not see them perform after they won those four silver sword awards at the Bronze Bardic Gala last spring.**

They only won three.

Oh, look who's keeping track.

"Would you remind me of your names and specialities?" the coordinator said, her eyes warily assessing us, unaware of our mental conversation. "It seems your guild forgot to write down that information when sending the recommendation."

Shit, we forgot to think of aliases, I spoke to Benny, giving the coordinator a smile that wasn't suspicious at all.

Allow me.

Benny, wait, just tell me your idea—

A high-pitched ringing pierced my ears as Benny linked our mental bridge to the coordinator's, something no other dragon in this godsdamn world would do because why talk to anyone other than their rider?

Having a dragon who loved people was annoying as shit, especially when we were trying to *not* draw attention to ourselves. If Benny or I slipped up and this coordinator found out we were here to kill Morally Gone, we'd fail the job and lose out on the bounty, which was quadruple the money this damn security personnel job offered.

Hello there! Benny spoke, his voice high pitched. *My name is Idyhnth, and this is my fearsome rider, Rosanna. We specialize in slaying aquatic monsters out in the fae realm, NOT to be confused with the bounty hunter duo Rhema and Arbentaliathoxian, who kill immortal men that abduct women.*

I shot Benny a glare. He gave me a quick wink.

Of all the aliases he could choose, of course it would be Rosanna—my fellow guild member, bounty hunter, and the woman who'd been driving me insane for years, and particularly the last few months.

And not in the good way.

"Right," I said through gritted teeth. "What he said."

"Ah, yes, wow," the coordinator replied, her voice shaky as she took a step back. "Well, according to the records your guild *did* successfully send over, you're not available for hire for the next two weeks due to requested time off."

My insides froze. That had to be wrong. Rosanna never had time for anything or anyone else except her bounties, and I knew this because she said it every time she had to miss a post-work drink or a guild-organized game night.

At least, that's what she told *me* every single time.

Oh, yes, that, Benny replied with a smile. *We had a last-minute change—turned out our paid time off was lower than we thought! You know us monster hunters, terrible at administrative work. Would do us some good to have someone like you around!*

The coordinator's face flushed as she twirled her foot into the grass. "Well, you know, it *is* a tough job. Hard to find appreciation for it nowadays."

Well, consider us your very favorite appreciators!

"I think she gets it," I interrupted, giving Benny's scale a firm slap.

He severed the mental connection with the coordinator, a small pop sounding in our mental bridge.

"Lovely, " the coordinator said with a bashful smile. "Now that we have that settled, we'll need you on bridge duty to start. After that, you'll be making rounds through the caves to make sure no brawls break out until the festival's over at dawn."

I raised a brow. "Bridge duty?"

"It's the means through which people arrive at the venue. They must cross the perilous bridge to reach the entrance of Courtchella: Beneath the Bluffs!" the woman explained. "Our headliner, Morally Gone, specifically requested it in order to build anticipation for their dangerous and dark new sound."

Don't you just love a good publicity stunt? Benny asked.

This band is more idiotic than I originally gave them credit for.

Even more so than the name of the enchanted diadem?

Do NOT sing your song about that damn thing, otherwise you won't be getting any butter balls during this job.

YOU WOULDN'T DARE.

I ignored him. "Alright, and let me guess: bridge duty

involves Ben–" I caught myself. "Idhynth and I catching the drunks who step too far wide?"

"Exactly! And then you'll make sure they safely get to the entrance and enjoy their night."

Right. A perfect system if I'd ever heard of one.

She handed me two bright-yellow tunics with a black cursive print of: *Ye Olde Security*. The edges were tattered, like moths had been chewing on them for years. With his freshly painted talons—bright purple and green to match the Morally Gone brand—Benny picked up his tunic and ripped it down the middle.

The coordinator's brow furrowed. I slapped my hand over my face.

He tossed the tunic around his neck, securing two of its half-eaten loops into his scales like wrapping a cape around one's neck. The two empty arm sleeves billowed in the wind with the *Ye Olde Security* font mismatched in the front.

I'm ready for bridge duty! Benny announced.

"I didn't think I'd hate this so soon," I sighed.

"Once the last person from the cliffside crosses, you may enter the festival." She handed me a scroll. "Here's the map so you won't get lost. You'll be paid at the end of the night."

I flipped open the map. Its inked depictions of unending curves, twists, and poor handwriting made it look like something Benny would write—not because he wasn't artful, but because writing with talons is nearly impossible.

Think your spelunking days can help us navigate this place? I asked him.

No worries, Rhemy. We'll be just fine!

If you say so.

Offering a salute to the cavern coordinator—knowing full well we wouldn't get any of *their* piss-poor coin after what we were about to do—I swung onto Benny and he stepped off the cliff. I clung to the leather reins and pushed my heels into the metal stirrups. Wind whipped through my half-shaven hair as we situated ourselves underneath the wide bridge, its stone pillars etched with glowing purple runes.

Are you serious? I finally said to Benny. *Rosanna? Idhynth? You couldn't have chosen anyone else?*

Are you still upset about when she had to rain check to go save that village from those pigmy goats that could pee fire? Because, honestly, I could understand the direness of that one.

It wasn't a date, I growled. *It was an after-work drink that she bailed on for the fifth time in a row.*

Oh please, it was more than that considering what day it was, Benny chided. **And may I remind you—the goats could pee FIRE!**

Then go have Helga take care of the godsdamn goats, not the bounty hunter who specializes in fae realm aquatic monsters.

Maybe Helga was busy. You know how it gets in the Nordic Realm—nasty business.

Or maybe Rosanna never planned on coming and she just didn't have the balls to say it.

To be fair, she doesn't have balls.

Thank you for that keen observation.

The first group of people walked across the bridge. Charms and enchanted lights were woven through their tattered and stained clothes, looking far more like a cry for a new hygiene routine than what Benny had sworn were the current "trends". Whatever the fashion was for these festivals, the temporary rune on everyone's forehead didn't match the aesthetic at all.

Benny sighed, returning me to our conversation. **Maybe Rosanna's going through something right now. There are many things you humans like to keep private that us dragons are still bewildered by.**

I guess I just thought— I paused, tapping a finger on Benny's gold scales.

Thought what?

I shook my head. Rosanna and I were bounty hunters, our

lives run by whatever jobs we could take. We didn't owe each other anything, especially what precious time we had outside of our work.

Nothing, I replied.

Thankfully, a woman's scream interrupted Benny's response. He shot across the lapping waves while I prepared to catch the falling woman. She landed with a light thud in my lap, wrapping her arms around my neck before she slid off into the ocean.

"Oh my gods," the woman hiccuped, her breath stinking of mead and mutton. "You just *saved* my life!"

I tried my best not to inhale her stench. "Wouldn't have to if you could hold your liquor."

The woman laughed so hard I had to tighten my hold.

"You're so funny!" she screamed into my ear, twirling her hair. "Am I going to see you at Morally Gone later tonight?"

"Let's hope not."

Rhemy! Manners!

Just get us to the cave entrance so we can drop this drunk lunatic off.

Not until you say sorry.

She should be the one saying sorry.

Fine, if you won't, I will.

Benny, stop—

The high-pitched ringing pierced our ears. **Hello very drunk woman, I want to apologize on behalf of my rude rider. She's very sorry and will happily see you later at Morally Gone.**

BENNY.

The woman's eyes brightened. "Is that your dragon?"

"What? Yes, but—"

"He can talk to me?!"

"No. Well, yes, but he shouldn't–"

"Is he telling the truth?"

"No–"

Of course! Now go ahead and enjoy the festival! He landed on the beach and pointed her towards the cave's entrance.

The woman had the same rune from the bridge marked on her forehead. I leaned forward to get a better look, but the inscription wasn't familiar. Her eyes lowered to my tits. As unwelcome as it was, I couldn't blame her for staring. They were looking rather nice in my new black leather armor, the design giving my tits some breathing room while covering my torso, arms, and neck.

"Since I saved your life, mind telling me what that rune is?" I asked.

"Rune?" she questioned, eyes still on my tits.

"Up here," I lifted her chin. "You've got one on your fore-head. What's it for?"

"It's Morally Gone's new logo and my proof of my ticket purchase for the festival." Cheeks blushing a bright red, she giggled and gripped my arm. "If you want to see a different mark on my body, I've got one just above my ass—"

"Alright, that's all I needed to know," I gently slid her off Benny.

She stumbled to the ground, laughing hysterically as she walked into the cave, waving at us until she disappeared into the darkness.

Something's wrong here, I growled.

Wouldn't be any fun if everything was right.

I gave him a side-eye. *Just help me watch out for more Morally Gone runes, hm?*

Whatever you say, Rhemy dearest! Now, who's ready for a song?

If you sing right now, I swear to all the gods—

Who sings like a sparrow
and soars like an arrow?
The bone to your marrow?

Arbentaliathoxian!
With voice so enchanting
And face e'er entrancing
Ass everlasting
Arbentaliathoxian!

To my dismay, Benny sang his song on repeat while we caught more drunk people, each interaction as annoying as the last, especially considering at least twenty of them were now expecting me to "meet up with them" at Morally Gone's performance.

Should we bet our last bit of coin on whether the final person will make it across? Benny asked.

Let's bet the rest of your butter balls.

Benny gasped. *You don't even like butter!*

I'm betting they're going to make it, I replied, ignoring his comment. *By the looks of it, they actually seem sober.*

And look at that footwork! Dancing just along the edge like they're toying with death. Just your type.

I do like a woman with a little kick.

Our laughter was stifled when we realized what was actually happening. The perfectly sober person charged forward, the opposite direction of where Benny and I were hovering, and *jumped* off the bridge.

Benny surged forward, his wings beating against the air. I dug my heels into the stirrups, adrenaline pumping through my veins: the woman was headed towards jagged rocks.

Faster, Benny!

Cold air whipped across my face. I ignored the pain while I stretched out my arm. But if I caught her like this, my shoulder would pop out of its socket.

New plan! I yelled. *We're doing Falling Goat.*

Oh, I love Falling Goat! Benny replied.

He maneuvered parallel to the woman. Gripping my axe, I

took one deep breath, then jumped. A new pain rocked through my body as I collided with her. She instinctively wrapped her arms around my neck. I grabbed my axe's hilt with both hands and sliced into the oncoming jagged rocks the woman had been falling towards, sediment raining down as we slid.

My arms, shoulders, and back screamed with pain, but I didn't let go. Instead, I gritted my teeth and squeezed my shoulder blades together, slowing our descent.

Any time now, Benny!

So impatient, he chided.

In one swift move, Benny soared underneath us. I bent my knees to absorb the impact as my boots met his scales. Finally my axe snagged in the rock and we came to a stop, Benny following suit. I yanked my weapon out of the stone and sheathed it, grabbing Benny's reins while keeping a tight hold on the woman.

Whew, what a whirlwind! Benny said, his flapping wings causing us to bob. **Well, Rhemy, since you bet she wasn't going to fall, I guess that means I won more butter balls after all.**

I swiped off the sweat dripping from my brow, ready to argue my way out of a bet I shouldn't have made, when I remembered the woman in my arms.

"What the actual fuck were you thinking?" I yelled at the woman, pulling her off me. "Trying to get yourself killed—?"

My jaw must've dropped because my mouth was suddenly getting sprayed with ocean mist. The woman stood a few inches taller than me, her dark brown skin complimented by her long, thin black braids, her deep brown eyes shimmering in the sunlight.

"I was *thinking* it would be fun to see if I could catch you and Benny off guard, but you two are just too damn good at saving damsels in distress," Rosanna said with a sly smirk.

A swirling heat wrapped around my gut. It'd been *months*

since I'd sat in that stupid fucking tavern, drinking pint after pint of ale, constructing excuses as to why she would be over three hours late. She'd promised she wouldn't miss it—dammit, it'd been *her* idea in the first place—and being the idiot I was, I had believed her. Then, one of her dumb enchanted letters had popped onto the wood bartop:

Goats peeing fire on a village. Going to take all night. I'll make it up to you next week, I promise.

I hadn't bothered to send a reply.

Rosanna! Benny shouted into our mental bridges, the high-pitched ringing causing my ears to fucking bleed.

Benny! she replied. *It's so good to see you, and I love the new talon color. Is that a purple and green combo I see?*

Oh, you noticed! It's to match Morally Gone's new album, Shadow Magic and Leather Jackets. *Rhema's really getting the hang of talon painting!*

"Truly?" Rosanna turned to me and grinned. "You? Talon painting? I didn't think you enjoyed art unless it involved using someone's blood as paint."

I clenched my hands into fists. Why the hell was she talking to me like this? As if everything was fine, as if she hadn't gone out of her way to plan a whole let's-have-a-drinking-game-night-together so I wasn't alone on the anniversary of my late wife's death, only for her to excuse herself with a godsdamn piece of enchanted paper? Like it'd just been an afterthought?

Like *I* was just an afterthought?

Maybe that's exactly what I was to her. And why wouldn't I be? We were just colleagues after all—colleagues that fucked one time two years ago on a random, drunk night. Nothing else had come of it. I hadn't *wanted* anything to come from it. So why the fuck would I start caring now?

"It was less about the art and more about avoiding one of Benny's infamous tantrums," I replied.

Benny smirked. *Works every time.*

I rolled my eyes. "Anyway, what are you doing here, Rosanna?"

Her smile faltered."Rhema, I—"

The sun suddenly felt scalding on my black leathers, my heart beating so fast I swore it was going to rip out of my chest. She gulped, a bead of sweat sliding down her cheek, collecting on her chin until it dripped onto Benny's back.

Was she going to fucking apologize while the sound of drunkards pissing on the beach echoed beneath us?

"Shit," she coughed, recovering her infectious grin, "sorry, what I meant to say was I'm here to offer my assistance."

My heart slowed, and something inside me deflated.

She continued, "Once I saw that you'd taken the Morally Gone bounty flyer off the guild board, I decided why not use some of my free time to help the one and only Rhema and Benny get their job done?"

That's actually the funny part of all this, Benny interjected, *we're not here as Rhema and Benny—*

My face flushed. *Benny, stop talking.*

We're actually using different names so no one at this event recognizes us in case they throw us out—

BENNY, STOP—

So we decided to pretend Rhema is you and I'm Idhynth!

Rosanna's brows raised to her hairline, her grin so wide I wanted to slap it off her stupidly attractive face. A part of me was grateful for the feeling—better anger than whatever the fuck had been welling up inside me.

"Identity theft," Rosanna said slowly. "That's a new one for you, Rhem."

"It was Benny's idea," I growled.

"Well, I'm honored we were the first to come to mind." She leaned in. "Sounds like my assistance was destined."

I flinched. "We don't need your help."

"But you need my name."

A silence pulled between us, a pleased look glinting in her eyes. Heat coiled around my gut. Her thin braids draped over her shoulders and down her curved hips. Despite her no-show at the tavern, I'd missed those hips, her lips, those fingers—

Shit.

I shoved her away.

"Where's Idhynth, anyway? Collecting a bounty while you frolic around Courtchella?" I asked, dousing the heat building in my body.

"She's at her favorite day spa. Benny knows the one."

Oh, yes, Fire Escape! Rhema, it really is the best, I should show it to you sometime. The frozen ice ponds are just divine. They even serve blood-and-butter flavored shaved ice!

"Excuse me?" I questioned.

What? Did I say something weird?

I ignored him. "Look, Rosanna, we just want to get this done quickly and quietly. So, if you could just go on your merry way, that would be great."

Rosanna smiled. "Have either of you been to Courtchella before?"

"Yes—"

No—

I glared at Benny. He gave me a huffed snort.

"I've attended nine times," Rosanna replied. "That cave system is bloated with crowds that'll keep you from reaching Morally Gone until long after their performance is done, but I know a way that'll take you straight to them in less than an hour."

That'd be AMAZING! Then we can really get some quality time with the band before we kill them—

"We don't need your help," I snapped. "We have a map, and as security, we'll be allowed access anywhere. I hope you enjoy your night off."

Benny landed on the shore. Rosanna let out a deep, dramatic sigh.

"What a pity," she replied. "Since you said you wanted this job done as soon as possible, I'd thought it would be the perfect remedy, especially since not doing your job as security personnel could get you reported before you even make it to Morally Gone. But that's my mistake for assuming. Have fun getting through those crowds!"

Rosanna jumped off with a brisk wave.

A handful of the drunkards we'd saved from the bridge were still stumbling towards the cave's entrance. They waved at us, yelling something about how excited they were to make out with me during Morally Gone's performance, their hoots and hollers interrupted by one of them puking on the other's boots.

Rosanna laughed. I glared at Benny. He gave me a purple talon thumbs-up.

Fuck my life.

Does that mean you're going to let Rosanna help us?

It means I don't want to be stuck in this godsforsaken place for longer than necessary, so if she's got a shortcut, then it would be stupid of us not to take it.

Even though she hurt your feelings?

She didn't hurt me, Benny... I just made a mistake and it cost me a good night's sleep.

Benny snorted. **Of course, Rhemy.**

I ignored him.

"So what's the catch?" I shouted after Rosanna. "You want my early bird special breakfast tickets from our guild's chef? Or maybe some coin to finally get you some desperately needed new armor?"

She turned, a hand on her hip. "How about a talon painting for Idhynth?"

We stared at one another for so long Benny started to hum his new theme song again. If we could get to Morally Gone before they started their performance, then it'd be one of the easiest bounty jobs we'd taken. No clean-up to worry about, no enchantment-hangovers to nurse, and more importantly, no sweaty drunkards groping at my ass. If Rosanna could get us there in time, then we could get our coin sooner than later, end up at a tavern, and I could drink my way into a relaxing week.

Guess it would be better to set the past aside than blow out my eardrums to tasteless music.

I'd just ignore Rosanna as often as possible. Easy enough.

"Fine, lead us to your secret passageway, or whatever it is, and I'll give Idhynth a talon painting."

Me too! Benny interjected.

Don't push it.

Rosanna smirked. "Sounds like a deal."

Yay! Benny yelled. *Ass up, face down, can't lose! That's our catch phrase by the way, Rosanna.*

"Oh, I need to know the story behind that."

Well, it was a couple years ago when Rhema was really drunk—

I ignored his and Rosanna's conversation, darkness falling over us as we entered Courtchella: Beneath the Bluffs.

2

___

LUSTY SHADOW MAGIC

MUSIC THUMPED THROUGH THE CAVE, rumbling with such force dirt fell from its ceiling. We'd been traveling along a softly lit path, the scent of the sea replaced with musty earth; a space somehow large enough to fit at least five full dragons—a fact Benny kept reminding us every few minutes while circling over our heads.

"So, do we know what we're dealing with down here with that enchanted diadem?" Rosanna asked, her twin swords shimmering in the orb lights.

"Of course–"

Not really, Benny sang.

I glared at him. He smiled and swooped around a stalactite. Cheers and shouts echoed along the cave walls, signaling we were nearing the main cavern.

"We *do* know what's going on," I continued. "The Diadem of Ancient Darkness and Devoted Yearning–"

She means the DADDY.

I let out a long, exasperated breath. "The *diadem* is used to enchant people and we need to stop it. Not much else to it."

Rosanna chuckled. "Then can you explain again how the enchantment works?"

"Does it really matter?" I asked.

Translation: we don't know, Benny chimed in again.

"Can you just shut up for three seconds?" I groaned.

Oh, because pretending we know what we're doing will help?

"We *do* know what we're doing."

Just because you said it twice doesn't make it true.

"Gods you're annoying."

At least I'm not a liar.

"You're lucky you're flying right now."

Oh no, I'm so scared! What will Rhema do, tap my scales with her axe?

"Why you little–"

"As entertaining as this is, we're about to be bombarded with a very obnoxious crowd and won't have a whole lot of time to plan," Rosanna stretched one arm over her head, then the other, muscles rippling in the light. "Even if we don't know how the diadem works, what about theories? Context? Clues?"

I slid my hand over my face. "You couldn't have asked for a briefing before you came?"

"You took the fucking flyer with all the information," she argued.

"Because you weren't supposed to be here."

Rhemy, go on and eat one of the dried meats I packed for you. I'll explain everything.

I rolled my eyes and, despite my annoyance, listened to Benny and my growling stomach.

What we know is that the DADDY's been missing for centuries and Morally Gone somehow found it, Benny explained. *The briefing also informed us they enchant anywhere between ten to twenty women at each of their performances, and the enchantments become permanent at midnight.*

"And what exactly happens when the enchantment becomes permanent?"

Benny swooped through another stalactite. *They become fans for life!*

"Translation," I spat, "we don't really know."

"Do you two always do this? Go into bounty jobs without a well thought-out plan?"

Rhema says we work best off of our intuition.

Rosanna laughed. I threw a dried meat stick at Benny's golden ass.

"Alright, so we've got your intuition and until midnight before they enchant a few dozen more women," Rosanna said, "Do we think these runes on everyone's heads have anything to do with this?"

I shrugged. "Probably."

Seems likely.

"You two are unbelievable."

"We know," I offered a beaming smile.

We turned a corner and Benny landed by our side. A large purple archway stretched over the entrance to the first cave, shimmering like a waterfall. A huge bald man with a black cloak and thin black goggles stood in front of the archway, chin tilted up. We shoved our way through the drunk Courtchella attendees. Each of the attendants ahead of us showed the bouncer the rune on their foreheads—the match of which was stitched into the bouncer's cloak.

The security guard traced each person's rune with his finger, the mark flashing from a chalky white to a glowing purple.

The runes are definitely a part of it, I spoke into Benny and Rosanna's mental bridge.

Why else would they be so creepy and aesthetic?

Exactly, Rosanna agreed, "So, I'll need you two to not fight for a *few minutes so I can do this right. I'm going to have to focus to get us in.*

I scoffed. *Look, I know you said you'd help us find a secret passageway or whatever, but we're the security personnel and this is the main cavern; getting in isn't a problem.*

It's not about gaining entry, it's about the passageway hidden inside that leads to Morally Gone's performance cavern, she explained. *Its location changes every year.*

And this guy knows where it is?

He's Morally Gone's personal bouncer. Of course he knows.

I turned to Benny. *Finding this passageway's going to be a waste of time.*

I think it sounds fun!

Of course you do.

Just play nice for a little bit and I'll get us the information, Rosanna instructed.

I rolled my eyes while Benny hummed his new song. Rosanna approached the man, her hips swaying with determined power, like a command for everyone to cease their thoughts and focus only on her. My head told me to look away, but my eyes refused. Dark brown skin shimmered in the purple archway's light, the outline of her ass accentuated by her tight leather pants. I had looked forward to seeing that ass two months ago.

Panic fluttered in my chest.

If she hadn't convinced me to go to that tavern for a godsdamn game night with her, I would've been fine. Benny and I would've found something to keep my thoughts off the anniversary of my late wife's passing. Instead, I was left alone, my grief searing into my skin and pouring down my throat with each swig of that putrid liquor–"

I cut our connection with her before you shared any of that, just in case you were worried, Benny whispered.

My face flushed. *Shit, thanks.*
Would you like us to leave?
I'm fine, Benny.
You're certain?
It's just a couple of rogue thoughts.

Benny furrowed his brow, tail wrapping around my feet. **Ok, but just say the word and I'll fly us out of here so fast you'll forget we came in the first place.**

I patted his scales in thanks. Rosanna lifted her halter top over her head.

Everyone in the line cheered at the top of their lungs.

"What the fuck?" I said, probably louder than I realized.

The bald man raised a brow, no smile in sight as Rosanna exposed her tits. He gave her a trite nod, no rune inspection, and whispered something in her ear. Giving the man a wide smile, she lowered her top.

Heat burned up my throat, my fingers curling into fists, a vision running through my head of punching the man square in the jaw.

Save it for Morally Gone, Benny chuckled.

I didn't reply as Rosanna turned around, winked, then disappeared through the purple archway.

"I'm *not* doing what she just did," I barked at the man.

He scoffed. "No need to, *Ye Olde Security*."

Waving us forward, he scoffed at our bright yellow tunics.

Remind me to come back here and beat his ass, I seethed.

Can I eat some butter balls while you do it?

Be my guest.

Benny whooped as we stepped through the archway and into the main Courtchella cavern.

Pink and green orbs of light floated along the cave ceiling, down the walls, and above the massive crowd. The smell of liquor and smoke wafted through the air, filling my lungs. I coughed, chest aching from the stench.

Rosanna grabbed me by the collar, the scar on her lip pulling with her wide smile as she dragged me forward.

"The passageway is on the other side of the cavern!" she yelled over the crowd.

"Great," I coughed, covering my surprise.

"So, did you enjoy that?"

"What? You flashing your tits in exchange for the secret passageway's location?" I replied. "You're insane."

"I'll take that as a yes."

Before I could argue, Benny's high-pitched ringing pierced everyone's ears, the crowd no longer cheering but shouting at what they thought was a blip in the music.

Excuse me, sorry, oh dear, sorry about your toe! Benny said to the crowd.

He was walking on his back legs, wobbling his way forward to keep up with Rosanna and me, the cave stalactites too low for him to fly. People's shouts turned into screaming delight, everyone cheering for the dragon who started to chat with them about which Morally Gone band member he loved the most.

Fucking fantastic.

A hush fell over the crowd as the lights changed to a deep magenta. Rosanna stopped, pulling me so close I could smell the sweat on her skin.

Lights glistened in Rosanna's eyes like a lake on a moonlit night. Small black curls swooped along her hairline, forming a swirled crown. She pushed her pink tongue between her teeth. A small smile widened on her full lips.

Time slowed, and I almost forgot about the lonely night in the tavern, the way my stomach had sunk when Rosanna's note appeared on the bartop.

I almost forgot, and damn me to hells because I swore I'd never do that.

Lute strumming blasted through the cave. I jumped,

turning away from Rosanna. A glowing boulder rose in the middle of the cavern, a large wooden arch decorated with flowers and vines curving over it.

A lone man stood on the rock, enchanted lights woven into his tattered green clothes. His long brown hair was somehow blowing in non-existent wind while he played his lute with such intimate vigor that I felt like I was intruding on something that really, *really* should've been kept private.

I can't believe it, Benny exclaimed into our mental bridge, his scaly tail swinging to the beat. *It's Tamii Quick!*

Who? I questioned.

Tamii Quick, Rosanna interjected. *He's a fae solo artist that got quite popular a few months ago. I'm surprised he doesn't have a bounty on his head yet.*

Why's that?

The music swelled until all I could hear were screams, the lute, and what I could only describe as a cracked cowbell. Tamii Quick approached an enchanted flower stalk and sang into it:

He dons black cloaks, I wear silk robes.
He's the Moon Lord, and I'm in the Rose Court.
Thinking about the day, where you shut up and find,
That what you're yearning for, is fucking me for your whole life.

Benny and I both let out a low whistle. Rosanna was right, this man had all the I-hate-women-because-I-can't-fucking-talk-to-them energy.

I didn't realize someone with such an extensive hair styling routine could still be a misogynist, Benny said.

Immortal men certainly are versatile, I agreed.

While Tamii continued singing his egregious song, we elbowed our way through the crowd and to the other side of the cavern.

"There it is!" Rosanna pointed, a faint shimmering purple door visible against the wall.

Just as we were about to squeeze through the last crowd of people, black smoke exploded into the cavern. The stench from earlier was replaced with an even worse smell: sandalwood and lavender.

Shadow magic.

I thought Morally Gone wasn't supposed to be in this cavern? I shouted into Benny and Rosanna's mental bridges.

They're not, Rosanna replied.

Well, lucky us! I smiled. *Looks like we don't need that secret passageway after all.*

Peeling away from Rosanna, I elbowed my way back towards Benny, his gold scales a guide through the smoke. I grabbed his reins and climbed onto my saddle, the attendees' bright purple runes the only things visible.

Beat your wings to clear the smoke, Benny.

But if I move the smoke, I'll ruin the whole atmospheric vibe! Benny argued. **The last thing anyone wants to be labeled as at Courtchella is a wet blanket.**

We're wearing security tunics. We ARE the wet blankets!

My worst nightmare has come true, he whined.

The black smoke began to swirl until its color shifted into a deep purple, the air turning thick and hazy. Everyone's runes shone a bright purple on their foreheads.

Shit. Is this enchantment happening?

Maybe?

I scrambled for answers, but this wasn't like anything we'd seen with shadow magic before. Benny and I had witnessed gross shadow tendrils that nonconsensually groped people, shadow magic that smelled like berries, anise, and cedarwood and acted like an aphrodisiac, but no shadow magic having to do with runes on foreheads.

Right, just start flapping your wings. We at least need to disperse the shadow magic so we can get a better sense of what we're dealing with—

A sweaty hand pulled on my arm with so much force I slid out of my saddle, reins slipping from my grasp as I landed on the crowd below. They scrambled for my hair, tunic, and even my fucking axe.

"Get off of me–!"

The strums of the lute were replaced by a loud rhythmic beat that drowned out my yells.

The runes glowed brighter on the attendees' foreheads.

A group of perfectly harmonized voices echoed into the cavern:

You can't see through my shadows
But I see through your soul
I'll take your breath like I'm the gallows
Break your mind and make you whole.

THE PURPLE SMOKE DISPERSED, giving way to six tall men wearing all-black attire. A few of them smiled, others smirked, and one of them didn't appear to care at all. They whipped their hair out of their faces in perfect unison.

Fresh screams erupted in the cavern.

Smell my musky leather jacket
Breathe it in like your last breath
Taste my lusty shadow magic
Take it all in it's depth
Breathe it in

> *Taste it now*
> *You're going, going*
> *Morally gone.*

TATTOOED, muscular, and a sheen of greed in their eyes, Morally Gone took over the stage.

"Oh my gods, it's Xzander!" the crowd screeched.

The undisputed leader of the group, Xzander, stepped forward, his leathery wings tucked behind his back. A silver diadem, with a glowing purple gem embedded at its center, sat atop his head.

"Welcome everyone, to Courtchella: Beneath the Bluffs!" Xzander exclaimed. "Can we all give Tamii Quick a warm round of applause for his delicious new song, 'You Wish You Could Fuck Me For Life'?"

Tamii dangled off the side of the rock, screaming like a small child. Xzander grabbed his arm and pulled him up and into a headlock, everyone cheering at the rescue. Tamii swatted at him uselessly.

The crowd's forehead runes pulsed with light.

Benny, burn them! I shouted.

There are too many half-naked people here, Rhema! I could kill hundreds of innocents.

Grinding my teeth, I shoved my legs and arms out of the crowd and elbowed my way to the stage.

Fine, I'll do it.

Rhema, Rosanna's voice shouted in my mental bridge, *don't get too close!*

I unsheathed my axe and screamed at the top of my lungs. Mere minutes in this damn place and I already stank like other people's sweat and my ears rang from the noise.

If only I hadn't charged at the stage so quickly, then I might've seen the warped sheen of an enchanted wall.

Thud.

The shield felt like a force stronger than a boulder had smashed into my chest. I yelled, slamming into people and collapsing on the cave floor, rocks digging through my leather armor and into my skin. Rosanna's familiar hands gripped under my arms, lifting me up.

"We need to run," Rosanna whispered into my ear.

"Not a chance. We need to kill them before this gets even more out of hand."

"Did you just say you want to kill us?" Xzander's voice echoed.

Everyone in the crowd stopped cheering.

Morally Gone's leader approached the edge of the boulder, dragging Tamii with him, the other five band members swaggering behind. The crowd whipped their heads towards us, eyes blazing purple.

Benny, phase two, NOW.

A slobbering man grabbed my arm. Rosanna and I batted it away.

But the attendees!

Another person grabbed Rosanna's hair, wrapping it around their wrist. I kicked them in the shin and she punched them in the gut. A swarm of enchanted fans staggered towards us.

THEN AIM IT AT THE CEILING.

Oh. That's actually a great idea.

A blaze of Benny's fire erupted into the cavern. Screams rose into the air as the enchanted shield shattered into a misty waterfall. Dirt and rocks fell from the ceiling. I lurched towards the stage, but Rosanna grabbed my arm.

"Let go of me," I yelled.

"This cave's going to collapse any second!"

"Do I look like I care?"

"I'm not going to let you get yourself killed for some bounty job."

"This isn't your assignment, it's mine, and I make the calls—"

Xzander's voice boomed through the collapsing cave. "Security, make sure those fake security personnel are taken care of. Everyone else, meet us in our performance cavern for the best night of your life!"

Morally Gone vanished into purple smoke, leaving Tamii Quick scrambling on the rock. I cursed. The crowd surged towards a huge gap in the cave wall while huge men in black cloaks and black goggles charged from the cavern entrance.

More security guards, and they were running towards us.

"We need to get to the passageway, *now*," Rosanna instructed.

"You've got to be kidding me!" I shouted.

Benny bounced onto all fours. ***Time to go!***

We grabbed his reins and swung onto the saddle. The shimmering purple door of the secret passageway wavered on the cave wall, its shine dimming with each step Benny took.

It's going to close any second, Rosanna shouted.

The bald man from the Courtchella entryway stepped in front of the dimming arch, two spears in his hand and a snarl on his mouth. He spun the spears around his head, behind his back, in front of his chest, between his legs, over his head again—

Can I burn him and get butter balls for it?

I'll give you five butter balls.

Five? This deserves at least eight.

Fine, six.

Eight.

That's not how bargaining works, Benny. You need to go one down.

I want eight or he lives.

I groaned. *Fine, eight butter balls.*

Yippee!

Before the man could attack, Benny melted the skin off his bones, turning him into ash. With a hefty push on the ground, Benny dove through the magic door, a loud pop bursting from behind us as it closed. Silence replaced the screaming fans. Darkness replaced the burning ceiling.

So, Benny said, *can I have my butter balls now?*

3

MEN LIKE DICKS MORE
THAN THEY LET ON

PURPLE AND GREEN orb lights flickered through the dark passageway. The scent of damp earth tasted like soil in my mouth. I turned around in my saddle, smoothing my hand over Benny's gold scales while he finished eating his butter balls. The entrance was gone, which meant the only way out was forward.

Maybe I should've been grateful it was closed, that we were cut off from the Courtchella guards and the enchanted mob. But, all I could think about was how close we'd been to killing Morally Gone and retrieving the Diadem of Ancient Darkness and Devoted Yearning. Just seconds away from completing this godsdamn bounty jobs and calling it a night. We would have been finished had Rosanna not got in my way with her "rescue" routine.

"Nice work, *guide*," I said to the back of her head.

She swung her leg around and sat backwards on the saddle, facing me. Her hips met mine and her folded arms pushed against my chest. If I wasn't so pissed off, I might've gotten distracted by the rip in her leather armor exposing the lily tattoo snaking up between her breasts and ending on her sternum.

Good thing I didn't care about that. Not one bit.

"It was obvious they outmatched us back there," she replied. "Better we escape and strategize before we go in for the kill."

"You've got to be joking," I said, the echo bouncing along the walls. "You think it's going to be easier to kill them once we're in the performance cavern?"

"Once we've devised a solid plan that doesn't involve running into an enchanted shield surrounded by enthralled fans, yes."

I raised a brow. "Tell me, what do you know about shadow wielders?"

Rosanna scoffed, her eyes darting to the ceiling. "What is this, a quiz? What I *do* know is that you were about to be crushed by falling boulders and I saved your life."

"Everything was fine, trust me. Isn't that right, Benny?"

Benny's loud chewing stopped. *I'm afraid Rhema's right. That was some of our cleanest work.*

He continued munching on his butter balls.

Rosanna waved her hands. "The entire cavern nearly went up in flames, Benny."

Benny and I looked at each other.

We've done worse.

"Way worse."

"Good gods," she breathed. "And I thought Idhynth was messy."

Annoyance burning in my chest, I grabbed her chin between my fingers.

"Since you have no idea what we're up against, let me lay it out for you," I began. "Morally Gone's performance cavern, or whatever the fuck this place calls it, is going to be a nightmare for us. I don't know how that fucking diadem works with those runes, but what I do know is that it'll be most powerful wherever they've decided to perform its enchantments. What this means is that the diadem will be far stronger, which means Morally Gone will be far more powerful, which means their enchanted fans will be even more psychotic, *and* their shadow magic will be near impenetrable."

In other words, it's going to be a pain in the ass to kill these guys AND get the DADDY, Benny chimed in.

"Come on, Benny, you're even more powerful than Idhynth," Rosanna said. "Surely this'll be an easy task for three bounty hunters to squash?"

Benny turned and blushed. *Rosanna, your compliments never cease to make me glow with joy.*

"It's because you deserve it, along with all the butter balls in the world," she sang back.

Did you hear that Rhema? Rosanna thinks I deserve ALL the butter balls in existence!

"Yeah, I heard her," I rolled my eyes. "Look, this is a *big* deal, especially with how many fans have those runes marked on their heads. If we don't get the diadem by midnight, who knows how many of them are going to be enchanted?"

But I thought they could only enchant a couple dozen people at most with the DADDY?

"Looks like they found a way around that," I replied.

I suppose they could be growing in power.

"Which could mean hundreds of people are in danger."

He snorted in agreement.

Rosanna straightened her back. "Then it looks like we either use this shortcut to get to their performance cavern or we sit in this dirt for the rest of our lives."

As much as I enjoy dirt, I'd hate to miss the new artisanal butters available this upcoming spring season. I've heard there's going to be a blueberry flavor this year!

"We wouldn't dream of letting you miss that," I scoffed and slid off his back.

Something squished beneath my boot. Yelling, I jumped backwards and unsheathed my axe. A being with long, tangled hair and an outfit interwoven with fairy lights sat up. They rubbed their head and cradled their jaw.

"Where's my lute?" they groaned. "Where are all my fans?"

I took another step back and realized exactly who this person was: the misogynistic performer who sang about how he wanted his women to fuck him and thank him for it.

Is that Tamii Quick? Benny asked, high-pitched ringing connecting all our minds.

"Of course it's me, you imbecile!" Tamii cried as he stood, grabbing his lute off the ground. "You're the ones who lit fire to my stage, aren't you? You're the ones trying to sabotage my fame?"

"Whoa, slow down there," I sheathed my axe and raised my hands. "We don't give a fuck about you, alright? We're here to get rid of Morally Gone. That's it."

"Morally Gone? Those freaks who stole my DADDY last month?"

I widened my eyes. "You found the Diadem of Ancient Darkness and Devoted Yearning?"

Tamii stole the DADDY?

"Of course I did! You think those shadow-obsessed idiots were able to get it themselves? Please." He scoffed. "After the woman I loved left me for a pathetic, useless man, I used the remainder of my magic to track down the DADDY. Of course, those fucking twats in the Star Flame Court had harbored it all this time. Why else would all those nineteen year old girls flock there like moths to a flame for centuries?"

Oh dear, no wonder we've had so many bounty jobs there.

I shrugged. *Suppose that was an oversight on our part.*

All the more reason for better plans, Rosanna muttered.

"I'm still telling my story," Tamil shrieked. "So, I used the remainder of my power to sneak into their court, steal the DADDY, and my fans grew by thousands until that stupid shadow boy Xzander raided my performance a month ago and stole it. So, if you're going to kill him and his little minions, then I'll just go ahead and take it off your hands so you can restore what's rightfully mine."

Benny and I laughed. Tamii frowned.

"Yeah, that's not going to happen," I said. "The diadem's coming back with us."

He stepped towards me. "You don't have need of it."

"And you do?" I bent down to his height. "What is it, Tamii? Can't get your fans without it?"

Tamii held his lute close to his chest. "You're going to find some way to bastardize it with your womanly ways and make it unusable for us men who deserve it!" He backed away slowly—carefully. "Well, I don't plan to just stand here and let you females do such a thing."

Tamii turned and ran.

"Females?" I remarked.

Rosanna leaned forward. "He really should have a bounty on his head."

Tamii tripped over a stone in the middle of the cave floor and slammed into the wall, a sound much louder than I'd expected reverberating through the cave. Purple runes brightened along the rocks. Scraping stone echoed through the cavern.

Pointed spears poked through the wall.

Sucking in a breath, I jumped away from Tamii and rolled next to Benny. The spears shot out of the wall, air rushing past my face, the weapons sticking into the rocks, bouncing off stone—and sinking into Tamii's head, stomach, and groin.

"I FUCKING HATE WOMENNNnnn..." His final shriek faded into the cave's darkness.

We all stared in silence, like we weren't sure whether what just happened had *actually* happened.

It happened, Benny whispered into my mind.

Benny, I know.

I turned to Rosanna. "So, not just a secret passageway, but a *booby-trapped* secret passageway? You're just full of surprises, aren't you?"

She laughed. "Sure, blame me for setting off all of Courtchella's alarm spells."

"Oh, so this is mine and Benny's fault?"

"I've been in here countless times and not once have I seen spears dart out of a fucking wall."

"Maybe if you'd just let me kill Morally Gone when they were right in front of me, we wouldn't be in this tunnel in the first place."

"Again, I saved your life, so you're welcome."

"Asshole."

"Prick."

Would you two stop flirting and look at the walls? Benny asked.

Rosanna and I grunted. Keeping a healthy distance from each other, we approached the wall, careful to not trigger the same stone as Tamii.

Did I eat expired butter balls, or are those dicks drawn with rune magic chalk? Benny asked.

I sighed, "Can't shadow wielders draw something besides vulgar images for once?"

I think a lot of men like dicks more than they let on.

"A truth all of them deny," Rosanna agreed, squinting at the wall.

Sure enough, there they were: glowing depictions of dick-shaped spears.

Why couldn't we get bounties with mature men for once? The last thing I'd want is to die by a penis-shaped shaft.

Look, Rhema, they even drew dicks with wings! Benny booped his nose against the depiction.

Blood rushed from my face.

Unsheathing my axe, I quickly backed away from the wall.

Rosanna huffed a laugh. "Rhem, what are you doing?"

I gripped my axe, eyes watching the shadows as a wave of nausea rolled in my gut. If those runes caused dick-shaped spears to appear out of the wall, then runes with winged dicks could only mean one thing.

Oh! I get it now.

"What?" Rosanna asked.

Benny laughed. ***I think we're learning how these runes finally work.***

A loud screech echoed through the cave. My blood turned cold.

The shadows shifted. I stepped back. Another screech sent the hairs up on the back of my neck. Purple eyes glowed through the darkness. A creature with large leathery wings and a long sleek snout swooped out of the shadows, its massive claws like short swords, its teeth like freshly sharpened spears.

All of those features I could handle—they were preferred, even—but the additional anatomy drawn by those godsdamn shadow wielders changed everything.

Hanging between the creature's hind legs was an abnormally large dick that swung in tandem with its wings, slapping against the ground and bouncing up to slap its stomach.

Fucking disgusting.

It tilted its head. Painful silence sliced into my gut, like a dark cloud before lightning struck. I tightened my grip on my hilt.

The bat lunged.

I sheathed my axe and ran.

"Benny," I yelled. "Kill it! Eat it! Do something and do it now!"

Come on Rhemy, I believe in you, Benny cheered across our mental bridge. *Face the big bat dicks like any other men you kill!*

Rosanna's laughter mingled with the bat's screeches.

I didn't dare turn around to glare, the sound of the creature's floppy member—like a stalker's footsteps—getting closer with each second. Another screech echoed in front of me. The dick-slapping sound doubled.

Fuck. Fuck. Fuck. Fuck. FUCK.

It wasn't that I hadn't come across stupidly big dicked monsters and men before. If anything, they were common when it came to our bounties. I was hired for our expertise in killing them. But stupidly big dicked monsters that could fly? Its ability to slap its disgusting thing in my face as an attack?

Hells fucking *no.*

I let out a grunt, pivoted, then flattened myself against the wall. A rush of wind whipped past my head. I dared to look up, the bat's dick swooping inches from my hair. I dove out of its path and slid across the cave floor, my leathers ripping and rocks scraping against my skin. Narrowly dodging another dick to the face, I ran back towards Rosanna and Benny who were doing nothing but keeling over in idiotic laughter.

"I'm going to kill you both!" I screamed at them.

Alright, alright. Rosanna, should we put Rhemy out of her misery? Split the difference?

She swung her swords in an arc. "Aw, but it's so fun watching her panic like this."

You're right. Another minute, then?

A big slap sounded at my heel. I pumped my legs faster. "Would you two just cut off their fucking dicks already!"

Rosanna grabbed Benny's reins right as he launched over me. I rolled to the ground, axe in hand. Benny unlocked his jaw and swallowed the first bat in one gulp. Rosanna swung off Benny's reins and wrapped her arms around the other bat's neck, slicing her blade across its throat. It let out a garbled screech, blood spewing through the air, warm drops of it splattering across Rosanna's face.

Her glittering eyes caught mine, a wide smile peeling across her mouth. As much as I wanted to hate that smile and ignore those eyes, I couldn't help but let the corner of my mouth turn up into a smirk. As the bat slowly collapsed to the floor, Rosanna's braids billowed behind her like a dark veil, the veins in her muscles straining with her hold.

A queen slaying her beast.

My heartbeat quickened, and my palms grew clammy, though the reason had nothing to do with the bat landing inches from my feet.

I would say you actually enjoyed these big bat dicks, Benny chided, the connection to Rosanna's mental bridge having been disconnected.

What about me running around and ordering you to kill them said "I'm enjoying myself?"

Benny pursed his lips. *I believe the answer is currently staring at you.*

Sure enough, Rosanna's eyes hadn't left my face.

I ignored his comment. *I'm just glad you actually came through and killed it instead of making me sprint for over an hour.*

It's not my fault you ran away like a little child instead of killing it with your big axe.

You know I don't like flying dicks.

They're more scared of you than you are of them.

Don't spew your bullshit at me.

He gave me a knowing look. I flipped him off.

"I'm sure you're both having a lovely chat, but maybe it's time we go and get your bounty?" Rosanna asked.

She held out a hand. I chewed my lip.

"Come on, Rhem, it's just a hand," she said.

But was it?

Instead of losing myself in a spiral of thoughts that Benny

would more than likely hear, I grabbed her hand, her callouses scraping against mine. She pulled me so close to her chest I had to lean back to not fall into her arms. Gulping, I slipped my hand out of hers and dusted off my leathers.

Let's take Tamii with us! Benny interjected into all our minds.

He's dead, I replied, *and bleeding.*

Please, Rhemy! What if he ends up coming in handy?

Rosanna and I paused.

"Just let him have his fun, Rhem," Rosanna said.

"Fine," I said, "but you're the one holding him, not us."

He smiled so wide he looked like he was about to sing. *Rosanna, you're the best! Now, let's go kill our boy band and retrieve the DADDY!*

4

RHEMA'S SCRATCHY SADDLE

TURNED out having a corpse covered in enchanted lights came with its perks. Not only was the dead musician's body decent in lighting a brighter path for us, but it ended up taking four more cock-shaped spears on our behalf, a few shadow magic darts, and even managed to function as a warning for the runic bats with big dicks.

Rosanna was sitting behind me, her chest flush against my back. Her toned arms wrapped around my waist and pulled against my stomach. I swore to the gods her pinky finger was roaming near my belly button, making lazy circles just above my waistband, but I couldn't be sure. All the bouncing from Benny's trot—the cave was too low for flying—made it impossible to tell if my theory was correct.

I ignored it because that was my plan for this bounty–not giving Rosanna any attention. It had nothing to do with the fact I might've slightly enjoyed it.

"Is this a new dragon saddle?" Rosanna hummed into my ear.

"Uh, yeah," I remarked. "Minotaur hide."

"Oh wow, minotaur? Far more durable than cow hide."

"Yes, well, that was the point."

Awkward silence stretched between us. Benny hummed his theme song from earlier:

> *Who sings like a sparrow*
> *and soars like an arrow?*
> *The bone to your marrow?*
> *Arbentaliathoxian!*
> *With voice so enchanting*
> *And face e'er entrancing*
> *Ass everlasting*
> *Arbentaliathoxian!*

"Wasn't your last one ox hide?" Rosanna asked.

My breath hitched. I didn't want to talk about saddles with her. I didn't want to talk about *anything* with her. I wished she'd fled with the crowd so Benny and I could finish this job by ourselves. If I ignored this menial question, then she'd know I was upset, and then she'd pester me further.

And I wasn't in the fucking mood for that.

"Buffalo, actually," I replied.

"Right, buffalo. I remember now."

More pained silence. More of Benny's distant humming. More of Rosanna's pinky finger aimlessly wandering around my navel. Heat burned the tip of my ears and sweat built along my neck.

"Was there a point to your question?" I finally asked.

Rosanna straightened. "I was just curious, is all. Last time I saw you, your saddle wasn't so scratchy so I wanted to know if you'd gotten a new one."

"It's not scratchy," I argued.

"Of course," she chuckled into my ear. "I just thought you really liked your old saddle. You always spent more time than anyone I knew cleaning and shining it. Always looked brand new."

I ground my teeth. "Well, when a saddle starts losing its reliable structure, it needs to be thrown out and replaced."

She paused. I grinned to myself.

"I'm just surprised you didn't get it repaired," Rosanna said slowly. "A replacement is a lot of coin and effort."

"Sometimes losing the coin is better than the fucking headache and patience needed for a long-winded repair."

So, help me catch up here, Benny spoke into only my mental bridge. *You two aren't talking about saddles right? This is about how Rosanna left you alone at that tavern two months ago on your late wife's death anniversary, and how you never replied to Rosanna's rain-check letter where she promised she would make it up to you, and now you're both trying to figure out what went wrong through this very odd saddle conversation?*

Benny, she just wants to know about my saddle, that's all.

I fear you're both more hopeless than I originally thought.

I shut down my mental wall, Benny's unhelpful and non-applicable advice disappearing with it. He bucked his head in annoyance.

"Rhema," Rosanna started, breathing into my ear. "If you let me, I can explain everything."

"Not sure what that has to do with saddles," I grumbled.

"You know what I'm talking about."

Gods, I wanted to lean into her, let her explain away why she left me all alone that night after promising she wouldn't let me endure it alone, my pathetic ass waiting and waiting and waiting—

I jerked forward. She'd already given me her reason. Besides, it hadn't been the first time she'd had to abandon one of our meet-up plans. Bounty jobs, Idhynth's lunch times, guild obligations—different excuses that made no difference from where I'd been sitting.

She'd made her choices, reasonable ones too, but I was never one of them.

"No need to waste any more breath," I replied. "So, how close are we to Morally Gone?"

Her fingers tightened on my hips. "Rhema—"

"Because I thought this was supposed to be a shortcut, but I'm starting to think you were given false information," I pushed.

She let go of my hips. "Don't be like this."

"Like what?"

"Like *this*," she motioned from my head down to the saddle.

I scoffed. "Oh, don't be *me*. Got it. Alright then, let's abandon this mission and go enjoy a spa day with Idhynth, hm? We'll let Morally Gone enchant people with that stupidly named diadem while we pretend nothing matters but our own agenda. Sounds more like your style anyways."

Her nostrils flared, her cheeks flushing a deep red. "Fine, let's just keep to ourselves and endure your scratchy-ass mino-taur saddle."

"Works for me."

Rhema, Benny's voice entered only my mind, *be careful.*

She should be careful. We're on limited time here and she's not focused.

Just take it easy. We don't know what she's going through these days.

Why the fuck are you always on her side? I asked.

Benny snorted. *Everything I say is always for your benefit, Rhemy. You know that.*

Do I? Because why in the hells are you taking her side when I cried so hard I fucking puked my brains out that night?

To be fair, you do that every other weekend.

But why take her side after I had finally listened to you, finally putting my trust in someone other than myself, only for her to take that trust and break it over and over?

Benny paused. *Earlier today you said she didn't matter to you.*

Yeah, well, I fucking lied. Happy?

A small gasp echoed through our mental bridge. Dammit. I should've kept my mental bridge shut.

Oh, so you DO have feelings for her!

I groaned. *If you don't shut your mouth—*

Benny cut me off. *Being self-aware is the first step to enlightenment according to my new book club friends, Rhemy! Continue down this path and you'll find everything you've ever hoped and dreamed for. Speaking of, if we get some of my dragon friends to buy the scale lotion my book club has been suggesting, I might be able to pursue my dream of entrepreneurship this year. Apparently, if we sell it to five of them and have them sell to five more, we'll gain favor with the head of production. Do you think Idhynth would be interested?*

Benny, is your new book club a fucking multi-level marketing scam?

What's that?

I slapped my face. *Remember the dragon cologne brand you found last year?*

That was a very different situation. They were mean.

How much coin have you given this book club?

They only asked for a small portion of our savings. But it's a worthy investment, trust me!

I groaned. *That's it, I'm reducing your access to our funds—*

The ground shook, sending a small shower of pebbles falling from the ceiling. I instinctively gripped Rosanna's wrist. She hitched a breath. I maneuvered my hand like I'd accidentally lost sight of the reins, which I *had*.

Benny's voice echoed into all our minds. *Well, that's concerning.*

"No shit."

After jumping off his back, I approached the cave wall to investigate. Rune symbols had been carved into the rock, these ones done with far more precision than the dick drawings from earlier.

Are these music notes? I asked.

Benny slid beside me, the dead musician hanging in his mouth slapping my face. I batted the bleeding corpse away while Benny squinted his eyes at the wall.

They are! Good eye, Rhema, I've taught you well. They look like they spell something: D-A-D-D-E-E, Benny sounded out. ***Oh, it's just referencing the DADDY!***

But what's that shape next to it?

Huh, if I didn't know any better, I'd say it was a—

Dirt exploded from the ground. A creature as large as Benny emerged, except it looked like a snake with a dragon-like face sliced with scars and spotted with horns. But where Benny's eyes spoke of emotion, these eyes spoke of animalistic hunger.

—*wyrm!* Benny finished his sentence.

A purple rune glowed on the wyrm's forehead, matching its vibrant eyes.

"I swear to the gods if this thing has a bigger dick than the bats, I'm going to torture that bardic boy band before we kill them," I muttered.

Does this wyrm seem familiar to you, or is that just me? Benny asked.

I turned to him. *We never fight wyrms.*

Benny paused. ***Hm, you're right. How odd.***

Rosanna stood on Benny's back, her twin swords unsheathed and spinning in consecutive arcs. "We're over halfway to Morally Gone's stage, so you two should keep going. I'll take care of the wyrm."

I raised a brow. "Considering we'll probably kill it faster together, this feels a bit dramatic."

"I've killed hundreds of these things. Trust me, it's my specialty."

"You've killed an enchanted shadow magic wyrm before?" I asked.

"How different can it be from regular wyrms?"

"This whole hero routine is getting old," I muttered.

"I think you'll feel differently once I get this job done." She winked.

Rosanna jumped through the air, her twin swords aimed at the wyrm's neck. The monster twisted its head away from her, as if it didn't even notice a goddess-like warrior soaring straight for its throat. She yelled in triumph, her blade inches away from its target.

Thwack.

The wyrm swung its tail, its scales hitting her square in the chest. She slammed into the cave wall with a thud.

Benny and I shuddered.

That's a rough one, Benny said.

Quite the bruiser, I agreed.

"I'm fine," she grunted, offering a wobbly thumbs-up. "Maybe you were right about the shadow magic."

"Glad you figured that out," I smiled. "Looks like Benny and I aren't the only ones who go in without a plan."

I unsheathed my axe and sprinted for the monster. It slid across the floor with fluid precision, neither a defensive stance nor an attacking move. In fact, it was a tactic that made no sense at all.

Rhema, duck! Benny yelled.

Collapsing to the ground, I dodged the wyrm's tail as it flew towards my head. Benny charged forward and the wyrm maneuvered in choppy patterns. Strange. The wyrm hadn't even looked at me when it swung its tail, nor was it looking at Benny whose throat glowed, readying for a fire attack.

Benny's flames erupted into the passage.

Shit.

I sprinted to Rosanna, who sat motionless against the wall,

using my body as a shield to protect from Benny's fire.Sweltering heat burned at my back, but I kept my composure, my black leathers resistant to the flames, except for the small tear I'd received from the bat attack. I gritted my teeth, the pain harsh and sharp. The fire reflected red-and-orange sparks in Rosanna's dark eyes, her chest heaving and pressing against mine. Sweat dripped down her neck, sliding along the exposed part of her collarbone.

She pressed her palm against my sternum, her fingers curling into the fabric. There was something desperate in her face, the way her brows scrunched and her lips parted, a loose strand of black hair framing her face. I wanted to fall into whatever trance she was dragging me into; wanted to feel her body the same way I had two years ago; wanted to admit that the last couple of years waiting for her had felt empty.

Lonely.

"Rhem," she whispered, "I'm sorry about what I said. Your new saddle isn't scratchy. It's just... different."

Breaths short, head spinning, I yelled at myself to step back, to give ourselves some room to breathe. I was supposed to be ignoring her. But *dammit*, I didn't want to, not when Rosanna was this close. Not when she was finally within my grasp.

I leaned in until her breath mingled with mine.

"I never wanted a new one," I whispered.

Her eyes dropped to my mouth. I traced my hand up her arm, all the divots and roughness from her scars catching on my callouses.

"Why didn't you respond to my letter?" she asked.

Visions of my late wife's goodbye letter flashed through my mind's eye. It was sweet and beautiful and tragic, nothing like Rosanna's. But, it hadn't felt any different, because the outcome had been the same: they'd both left me alone.

I pushed off the cave wall. "Because I knew you were busy, just like I was."

Rosanna tilted her head. "You don't need to lie to me, Rhem."

"I'm not," I assured her with a false smile. "I was fine."

She furrowed her brow.

Uh oh, we might have a problem, Benny whined.

Fighting the pull in my body, I ripped myself away from Rosanna. The passageway smoldered, rocks crumbled from the ceiling, and smoke swirled through the air.

Yet the wyrm remained unscathed.

"How the hells did it survive that?" Rosanna coughed.

"Fucking shadow magic," I muttered.

The creature resumed its sliding and chopping motions. It wasn't attacking us, which was confusing, but it wasn't letting us pass either. If Benny's fire couldn't kill it, then what could?

The moment I asked the question, the answer became all too clear. It seemed to hit Rosanna too, because her confusion turned to laughter.

I really fucking hated this job.

It's dancing to the choreography of Morally Gone's new hit song, "Shadow Magic and Leather Jackets"! Benny's voice grew in excitement with every word. *Alright, follow my lead and we'll kill this wyrm—together.*

I groaned. *I'm not going to kill this monster with choreography.*

Oh Rhemy, good choreo is the only way to kill it.

Rosanna grabbed my hand, and we joined Benny in front of the dancing wyrm. Benny recited every single choreography step: Hand on hip, lean left, jazz hands, hop twice, and so on. Rosanna followed him, the two of them laughing uncontrollably.

It made me sick.

Instead, I jabbed at the creature with my usual attacks. Slashes to its scales, an attempt at cutting its jaw, even a punch to the gut, but the wyrm had a finesse I'd never witnessed before in man or monster. It blocked, dodged, and managed to get multiple hits on my chest and shoulders. Rosanna and Benny remained untouched, inching closer to the monster's throat.

Finally, begrudgingly, with every hateful fiber in my body, I listened to Benny.

And I fucking danced.

Chest pop!

I obeyed. We all avoided a sneak attack to our backs.

Hip sway and step forward once, twice, three times!

Rolling my eyes, I followed his instructions until we were inches from the wyrm's neck.

Now jump and lift your heels!

Lift our heels—?

JUST DO IT.

We all did it, striking the wyrm right in the throat–Rosanna and I with our blades, Benny with a single talon. The scales lit a bright purple, the force from the hit reverberating through our hilts and into our arms. A drawn-out roar trembled through the cavern. The wyrm's purple rune vanished, the creature swaying until it collapsed to the ground.

Rosanna laughed. "Are your bounties always this fun?"

You and Idhynth should join us more often! Then we can have our own little dance parties after we finish our bounties.

"Oh, we'd *love* that."

"Sure you would," I grumbled.

Panting from all the footwork, we grabbed our weapons and continued through the passageway until a high-pitched ringing pierced our ears.

It was different from Benny's: lower, more controlled. I unsheathed my axe again and cracked my neck.

Arbentaliathoxian, did you just break the enchantment on me? a low, melodic voice sounded in our mental bridges.

The wyrm turned its attention to Benny, its eyes no longer full of hunger, but sparkling in Tamii's enchanted lights.

Benny let out a laugh. *Gegraz! By the gods, I knew you looked familiar! Thousands of years old and still spritely as ever.*

I held up my axe. "Sorry, you two know each other?"

Benny replied, *Remember when I told you I used to go cave-spelunking? Gegraz was one of my adventure partners!*

I stared at my dragon like he'd lost his fucking mind.

Gegraz chuckled. *Those were the days, weren't they Arben?*

"Arben?" I questioned.

"Idhynth's got a few nicknames from her past, too," Rosanna said with a quick elbow jab. "My favorite of hers being Inny."

"Alright, Inny's cute, but... *Arben?*"

We chuckled, a welcomed respite from the building tension.

That they were, Benny smiled. *Oh, Rosanna, could you wipe some of that blood off Gegraz's throat? I feel so terrible for doing that.*

"Of course," she replied, grabbing her swords and sheathing them. "Sorry for almost killing you, Gegraz. My dragon, Idhynth, and I have never met a sentient wyrm in the fae realm."

Oh, fae realm wyrms? I hate them and their snooty little snouts. Best to kill them all.

"Oh." She gave me a wide-eyed look. "That's a very strong opinion."

Gegraz shrugged—I think. Hard to tell without shoulders.

So, did Morally Gone put you under that enchantment? Benny asked.

Oh yes, those boys are very sweet. Stupid, but sweet. They use that enchanted diadem of theirs to lead all the rats my way. In exchange, I had to become a mindless monster the past few days and kill trespassers from time to time. Nothing like some human flesh to keep the old brain functioning!

"What?" Rosanna and I said.

Don't fret, little beans. Any friends of Arben are friends of mine.

"Did he just call us beans?" I whispered.

"He does live under a very large rock," she muttered.

Benny sighed. *I've always tried to tell Gegraz it would be better for his digestive tract to just eat vegetables and rabbits.*

And I've always told him it's far too bland of a diet.

That's what butter is for! Did you know they make flavored kinds now?

Do they? Tell me, what kinds?

I interrupted before Benny gave us a three hour lecture on different butter variations. "Since you were able to break through your enchantment, Gegraz, does that mean Morally Gone's enchantment on the fans can be broken after midnight?"

Gegraz laughed. *If a human has the fortitude of a centuries-old wyrm, then I don't see why not.*

"Great, so that's a no," I sighed. "While this reunion is very, uh, *interesting*, we have to go before Morally Gone permanently enchants hundreds of people tonight."

Hundreds? Gegraz asked, *Oh, little bean, they intend to brainwash everyone who bears a rune on their head. Their stage has a rune etched in it so large, it'll be able to enchant thousands.*

I furrowed my brow. "There's no way these idiots learned how to expand the diadem's power in such a short time frame."

The DADDY is one of the most powerful objects I've come across in centuries, Gegraz replied. *You shouldn't underestimate what it can do.*

"Then we better hurry."

The air turned cold. Gregaz hummed something eerie, his presence slithering around our mental bridge.

You intend to destroy it, Gegraz whispered, a dark threat weaving through his voice.

I steadied my axe. Rosanna gripped my wrist, motioning for me to back down.

Benny stepped between me and the wyrm. *Gegraz, the boys*

may be sweet and stupid, but they're actually hurting a lot of people with that diadem. I mean, look at what happened to you, dancing without your own knowledge!

Gegraz shrugged again. *I rather enjoyed it.*

Benny sighed. *I know being enchanted can be entertaining from time-to-time, but it's far more dangerous for humans. They're entire short lives could be stolen from them.*

The wyrm snorted. *But if you destroy the diadem and kill the boys, where will I get all my rats?*

Benny gently placed a claw on his tail. *Gegraz, you know you never needed the rats.*

They stared at one another for an unbearable amount of time. Gregaz's eyes started to water. A single tear fell down his scaly face. I gave Rosanna a what-the-hell-is-happening look. She replied with a pouted lip that said who-the-fuck-knows. I laughed.

Whatever tension had formed between us earlier had eased. It was a good thing, too. My emotions had been getting the better of me—distracting me. Rosanna was and always would be a colleague who had every right to live her life, whether it included me or not. I should be grateful she decided to join us for the bounty tonight, because that's all this was.

All it could be.

You're right, Arben, how could I have forgotten? Gegraz said through a few sniffles.

Let's go spelunking sometime soon, for old time's sake?

Yes, I'd like that.

Waving goodbye with his head, Gegraz returned to his hole, wishing us luck and issuing a warning: the closer we were to the diadem, the stronger its power would be. We thanked him for the help, I gave Benny a handful of butter balls, and we continued through the tunnel with Tamii's dead body lighting the way.

5

BLACKCURRANT ABSINTHE

An unnecessary abundance of cock-shaped spears and big-dicked bats greeted us on the last stretch of our journey to Morally Gone's performance cavern. Benny didn't mind having the bats for dinner as long as I awarded him a butter ball or two for every bat he ate—otherwise, he'd let the bats torment me.

And those motherfuckers deserved to *die*.

The passageway had expanded enough for him to stretch his wings and fly through its remaining twists and turns, his bat-eating looking more like a child catching bubbles than a vicious dragon ripping creatures in half. Not only was Benny eating bats, but he refused to let go of the dead musician, Tamii Quick. I'd had no choice but to tie the corpse around his neck like a fucking pendant.

We didn't have time to suffer one of his godsdamn tantrums.

I held tightly to his reins, squeezing my thighs for balance through the occasional twists and turns. Rosanna gripped my waist, her fingers digging into my hips, her infectious laughter at Benny's antics singing in my ears.

Fucking torture.

Not in the this-is-so-annoying-shut-the-fuck-up kind of way, but in the I-want-to-turn-around-and-kiss-you-until-I-forget-the-world-exists kind of way, which made no sense considering I'd firmly decided mere minutes ago to be colleagues with her. Had I thought that would suddenly make her ugly or something? Like she wouldn't still look or sound like a fucking goddess?

Gods, this would be harder than I thought.

Oh, Rhema's got it bad, Benny chided into my mental bridge, having disconnected from Rosanna when we'd lifted off the ground.

Can this wait until we've killed the bardic boy band?

There's no better time than the present to figure out your sexual feelings!

There's never a good time for that.

He ignored me. *Now, you want to fuck her, right?*

I'm not answering that.

Great, so you do.

I hate you so much right now.

Benny continued, *There's no need to try and talk yourself out of these things, Rhemy! Just accept this is how you feel and that you'll find someone who'll show up when you need it.*

I gulped. The idea of that *not* being Rosanna made my chest ache.

Benny's tone softened. *Or who knows? Maybe Rosanna will be more available after this?*

How many times had I thought something similar? That next time would be different? That Rosanna would show up? I'd hoped and wished for things to change—stuck in my own cycle of insanity.

The final straw was the night of my late wife's death anniversary. It had to be.

Just because she showed up to help us, didn't mean I would

forget or forgive the pain she caused. I was done letting her indecisiveness fuck with me.

Waiting for her to change might just kill me, Benny, I replied.

His tone softened. ***It sounds like you want more than just to fuck her.***

I shrugged. *Maybe I do.*

We flew in silence, save for Benny's methodical chomping of the bats.

Well then, he whispered, ***she doesn't know what she's missing out on.***

A small smile worked its way along my mouth. *I'm not too sure about that one, but thanks for the boost, bud.*

Benny let out a hum. ***Sounds like the perfect time for me to distract you with my newest song!***

That's really not necessary—

What sparkling jewel upon this crown
Dost gathers darkness all around?
And like the moths before the flame
Calls out to maidens the sacred name?
D-A-D-D-Y
Daddy tells them, "Don't be shy"
D-A-D-D-Y
Daddy no one can deny

As if on cue, a bright purple glow erupted through the passageway. Intricate runes wrapped around the cave from floor to ceiling. Benny came to a halt and hovered, his red eyes glinting in the light with pure wonder.

A shimmering purple doorway lined with statues was straight ahead.

"Come on, Benny, let's get out of these runes. Looks like we found the entrance," I urged.

But isn't it just so beautiful? No dicks, just pretty swirls, flowers, and what looks like berries! He crooned. ***It even smells good.***

"Now isn't the time to get distracted—" I paused. "Wait, what do you mean it smells good?"

Benny turned to look at us. ***Uh oh.***

"What's happening?" Rosanna questioned.

"Shit."

Pink and purple smoke exploded from the runes, the air smelling like anise, sweet berries, and warm cedar wood. I covered Rosanna's nose and mouth. She fought against my hold and ripped my hand away.

"You can't breathe *any* of this in—" I instructed.

But I was too late, Rosanna's chest expanding as she took a deep breath in.

"Why? What is this?" She asked.

Good fucking gods.

"This is blackcurrant absinthe shadow magic, a type of poison Benny and I have worked our asses off to be immune to. But since you just chose to not listen to me, you've now been infected with one of the most powerful and deadly aphrodisiacs in shadow magic history. Congratulations."

Rosanna's eyes rolled to the back of her head. I grabbed her and slid off my saddle.

"Benny, are you able to fan this shit out of here?"

You bet I can!

"Good, do it quickly. I need to double back and find a spot where it's clear so I can give her the antidote."

Think she's gonna agree to eat that thing?

"She doesn't have a choice."

All I'm saying is that she's just as stubborn as you.

"I can handle her stubbornness," I argued. "Now get to it so we can clear this out for her."

I ran back the way we came while Benny flapped his wings to clear out the smoke. Boulders and rocks jutted from odd angles. I jumped, skipped, and stumbled around them until the air finally smelled like dirt instead of musk.

Finally, I found a small alcove with a conveniently seat-shaped rock. After setting her down, Rosanna twitched so violently she punched me in the face.

"Fuck," I spat, rubbing the dull ache on my cheek, "was that really necessary?"

She opened her eyes. The orb lights reflected in them like stars, searching me face like she was desperate to find something.

"I have so much to tell you," she whispered.

Air rushed out of my lungs. "What do you mean?"

"I—" She shook her head. "Rhem, I'm—"

She stopped herself, a heavy silence stretching between us. Her eyes widened, that deep brown gaze sliding down my face, lingering over my mouth, and stopping at my neckline.

I shut my connection to Benny before my thoughts got out of hand. Blackcurrant absinthe was already a powerful aphrodisiac, and thanks to the diadem, this particular dose could be fatal. I had under ten minutes to reverse its effect. Whatever she wanted to tell me would have to wait, no matter how badly I wanted to hear it.

I broke the silence. "Look, you're going to need to do something for me, alright?"

Voice breathless, she said, "Just say the word, Rhem."

For fuck's sake.

I searched through my pockets for my herb bag. Once I found it, I pulled out a pink rose petal and rubbed powdered turmeric into it. Then, I threw the mixture into my mouth and chewed.

Rosanna's pupils dilated. Heat rushed up my throat and into my face. I hadn't meant to look, but it was hard to avoid her with the way her fingers crawled up my arm and smoothed over my bicep. I spat the herb into my hand. Her front teeth snagged on her lower lip, that light pink color of her mouth exposing itself.

Shit.

More heat ran through my body, pooling in my stomach—my stupid-as-fuck pussy starting to think a lot louder than my brain.

"Eat this," I said, handing it to her.

She observed the chewed-up antidote and tilted her head. "No."

Blood rushed from my face. "You said 'say the word' and I did. Now eat it so you don't die."

A mischievous smile pulled across her mouth. "I don't feel like I'm dying."

"You are, so take it *now*."

Pressing it into her palm, I waited for her to get it over with. She smiled at it, then, she gave it back.

"Put it in your mouth again," she demanded.

"I don't need the cure, you do."

"I *will* eat it, but only if you do what I say."

"What?"

She raised a brow and leaned forward, her nose inches from mine.

"Put it in your pretty mouth," she paused, her eyes moving to my lips, "then I'll eat it."

Every nerve in my body lit up in flames. Hands shaking, breaths quickening, I couldn't stop my tongue from wetting my lips. I knew what I was feeling, knew I wanted to grab the back of her neck and kiss her until it hurt. But I couldn't—*wouldn't*. She needed the antidote, and I needed to stay in control for that to happen. So, I did the only thing I could think of to get the herb in her mouth:

I fucking tackled her.

Our limbs tangled, her skin brushing against mine. I pinned her wrists on the cave floor. Unfortunately, the poison had done nothing to reduce Rosanna's strength. Smiling, she crushed her knee into my gut. I coughed so hard my lungs hurt. My grip loosened, and she broke out of my hold.

"It's always so sweet when you try to out muscle me," she crooned.

"Just shut up and do what I say, you stubborn little shit," I coughed.

She gasped. "Don't go stealing my lines like that, Rhem."

Maybe I knew this would happen, and that's why I tackled her. Maybe I knew if I tried to go strength-for-strength with her, I'd inevitably lose, and if I lost, that meant she had me.

And gods knew she only ever listened when I was under her.

With a force so swift and intense I swear my vision went dark for a moment, Rosanna flipped us, slamming my back onto the cave floor and anchoring me down with her thighs on either side of my waist. One of her hands pinned my wrists above my head, the other swiped the herb from me.

"So, are you going to finally open that pretty mouth of yours?"

Sweat slid down my temple. "Why do you always have to make things so difficult?"

"Because getting you flustered is one of my favorite pastimes."

There was no escape. Her grip was solid—immovable. I might've specialized in killing powerful immortal men, but Rosanna slayed monsters three times her size. There was only one way out of this, and I wish I could say it was difficult for me to do:

I let her have me.

She smiled. "That's my Rhem."

Slowly, she brought the chewed herb to my lips, pushing it into my mouth with her finger.

Shit, shit, *shit.*

I wanted to lick that finger, suck on it, hear her moan from it. Instead, I took a deep breath through my nose and closed my eyes until only the herb was in my mouth.

"Now, put it in mine," she instructed.

As I went to release my wrists from her grasp, she held them fast. I furrowed my brow.

"Not like that."

The soft skin of her nose brushed along my cheek, her hand leaving my wrists and sliding up my neck.

"Ros-Rosanna," I gulped, "the blackcurrant absinthe—"

"Is the most poisonous aphrodisiac," she whispered, her lips brushing along my throat, that soft voice gone. "So you better use that mouth of yours to stop it."

This godsdamn woman, always so fucking demanding when horny. There was no world in which she was going to concede to anything I said at this point, so there was only one way to do this without getting her caught in whatever shadow magic devoted yearning web Morally Gone was weaving.

I grabbed her scarred chin between my fingers, tilted her full lips to mine, and pushed my way into her warm mouth. Her tongue slid against mine, graceful and smooth, and her fingers traveled up my thigh. A spark shot down my chest and in between my legs.

I needed this—her. Despite never having the right words to explain my feelings, my body always knew. No one else could touch me the way she could. I didn't want anyone else the way I wanted her.

Fuck.

I pushed her off. "There, you have it now."

Opening her mouth, she winked. The herb was sitting on her tongue, but she didn't swallow it.

"How about I make a deal with you," she said, "if you come, then I'll eat it."

A mix of want and anger curled in my stomach. I didn't

know exactly how much longer she had until the shadow magic would take her, but I knew it was soon. That, and Benny had been right: she was stubborn as all hells.

"How about you stop fucking around so I don't lose you?"

I swung my leg over hers, flipping us again so I was on top of her. Surprise lit her eyes.

"Swallow it," I demanded, unsheathing my axe and placing it against her throat.

She smiled. Her forehead sparked with a purple glow, the faint outline of the Morally Gone rune appearing on her skin. "Make me."

Panic and desire spiked through my veins. We were out of time, and I was out of options.

"Stubborn asshole," I muttered.

Sheathing my axe, I pushed my finger into her mouth, forcing the herb into the back of her throat. She sucked me deeper into her mouth, wet tongue swirling around my finger. A whimper left my body as she arched her hips against my groin.

Breaths quick and heart racing, I commanded her to swallow. She shook her head. I gripped her throat, demanding it again. Laughing, Rosanna took my hand and ripped it off her neck.

"Say it the way I like it." Her tone was so smooth, so sultry, I almost came undone on the spot.

This wasn't the scenario I'd imagined for us considering she was about to die from shadow magic poison *and* I'd been purposely ignoring her for months, but I'd be lying through my godsdamn teeth if I said I wasn't enjoying this.

Lowering my voice, I said, "Please, Anna. Swallow for me."

She bit her lip, and then, she finally obeyed.

With a quick jolt, she spun us again, taking advantage of my lowered guard. Balance off from trying to get her to swallow, I couldn't stop her from slamming me down again with her thighs. Her black braids fell down to the floor, curving over her gorgeous tits.

The glowing purple rune dissolved from her forehead, leaving a white outline behind.

"Ah, I feel much better," she crooned.

Unsheathing one of her two swords, she twisted the bottom of the hilt. My thoughts journeyed away from her rune-marked forehead to her dexterous fingers. She popped off the hilt, and what slid out of it had me groaning and writhing underneath her.

"Rosanna," I breathed, fighting the pleasure building in my core, "you need to stop carrying your stupid crystal dildo in your sword's hilt like that. Someone's going to find out what a freak you are."

"Then let them." She smirked. "Besides, it's a cleaner alternative to using my fingers, and I'd hate to give you anything other than a good time." She leaned forward. "Now, be a good Rhem and take off your pants."

"But Morally Gone—"

"Is just on the other side of that door. Besides, I thought you liked having last-minute plans?"

Muscles glistening with sweat, lips plump and just waiting to be kissed, Rosanna had me exactly where she wanted me. Despite my anger towards her, did I still dream about moments like this? All the damn time. Even though it hurt like hells when she hadn't shown up that night, had I soothed myself to sleep by imagining her warm voice in my ear? Imagining she was asleep by my side instead of the cold pillow next to me?

Yes. I had.

Restraint be damned. She was in control, and gods help me because I fucking wanted her to be.

I obeyed her, wrestling against my damn fighting leathers until I piled them underneath my naked ass. She grabbed my thighs and licked her way up to my center. Dark spots popped in the corners of my vision, pleasure winding up tight in my core. She grazed the crystal dildo along my center. I moaned, trying to keep it from echoing too far in the cave. Then, she slid it inside me.

"Fuck you, Rosanna," I yelled, and this time I didn't give a damn who heard.

"That's it, Rhem," she hissed, pushing it in and out of me, "Keep screaming my name, the one you love so much you used it to get into Courtchella."

I did love her name. Fuck, I loved feeling her breath on my skin, her laugh in my ear, her fingers on my waist, her tongue in my mouth. Whoever I was at the start of all this was gone. Defeated. Ruined. That responsible, restrained, dignified Rhema had been turned into nothing but a puddle of hedonism. Only Rosanna could get me to scramble like a godsdamn animal, send me to my knees, and have me praying I'd be made into a living sacrifice.

"Say my name," she commanded.

"Rosanna," I said through rough pants.

"No, I want you to say my name the way I like it."

I caught her gaze. "Anna."

Her eyes darkened. Heat and want curled into tight sparks at her touch.

"Shit," I moaned, "how the fuck am I already so close?"

She stopped and pulled it out. I cried in frustration.

"Should I stop?"

I should say yes. We were wasting too much time.

"No," I whimpered.

She pushed her tongue between her teeth, brushing her lips along my ear. "Then get on your hands and knees and say my name. *Now.*"

"Yes ma'am."

I said her name again. And again. Each time I did, she sent the dildo inside me: rhythmic, dutiful. She slid her hand between my thighs and rubbed my clit, timing it with each thrust. I lost all sense of where I was, screaming her name louder, the build-up excruciating. I'd been wanting this for so long. Not just for anyone to do this to me, but for Rosanna to be the one.

A small tap knocked on my mental bridge.

"No," I begged, "not again—"

Benny's talon crashed into my mental wall so hard it shattered on impact.

Rhema! Rosanna! Wow, I don't know what's been going on but it's been VERY hard to get into your mental bridges! I just cleared all the shadow magic so we can get through Morally Gone's back-stage. How's Rosanna coming— He paused. *Rhema? Are you doing what I think you're doing?*

BENNY, I yelled, *OUT, NOW.*

NOT AGAIN, he whined. *Why does this always happen to me—?*

I shut my mental bridge, but it was done. Finished. Every ounce of pleasure wasted. Groaning in frustration, I turned around to find Rosanna laughing, the dildo covered with, well, *me.* I wrestled my pants back on while she wiped down her crystal dildo with a spell-bound "clean" handkerchief she'd gotten at a festival a few years ago.

"On a scale of one to ten, how often does that happen?"

I gave an exhausted smile. "At this rate, ten."

"Maybe we'll get it next time." She winked. "Guess it's time to finally kill those bardic boys, huh?"

"You're going to need to stay here."

"What?"

I took a deep breath and rounded my shoulders. "There's a runic mark on your forehead now; though you're not currently enchanted, I don't want to risk you falling under the diadem's power when we fight Morally Gone."

"Good thing I just ate that herb, then."

I shook my head. "It's enough to counteract an initial dose of the blackcurrant, but not enough to prevent the rune enchantment from enthralling you."

"So you want me to just wait here? Alone? Rebraiding my hair while you and Benny go do the dirty work? Now I just feel like you're trying to steal all the fun."

"Look, I want your help in there too, but we can't keep you safe while we fight."

"I'll wear a mask or something—"

"No, Rosanna." I stepped close to her. "You killed the bats with big dicks because that's your speciality. This is mine."

Benny's high-pitched ringing pierced my ears. *Uh, hi you two, shouldn't we be going—?*

"To be fair, I've never killed bats with cocks *that* girthy before," Rosanna cut in.

I shook my head and ignored Benny. "You're a monster bounty hunter—you know your way around monsters, doesn't matter if they have small or girthy cocks. Immortal men are different—trickier. It was dumb enough of us not consider their use of blackcurrant absinthe. So please, I need you to either wait here or go home."

"Go home? You wouldn't have even gotten here without me."

I scoffed. "I would've killed them back at Tamii's stage if you hadn't been there to stop me."

Again, we're on a bit of a time crunch right now—

"Well then, maybe you should've thought of that before you brought me with you."

"I never wanted you to come!"

She opened her mouth, but she paused.

"That's not what I meant," I groaned, scrunching my eyes shut.

"No, you're right. You didn't want me here, you'd made that very clear from the start."

"No, I didn't mean it—"

"Then what are we *doing*, Rhem?"

"A fucking bounty hunting job, Anna. That's all this ever was!"

Silence, thin and fraying, pulled between us. Her eyes turned glassy, lower lip trembling. I furrowed my brow and clenched my fists.

Butter balls, more bad timing, Benny said.

"What do you even want from me?" I whispered to Rosanna.

She stilled. "What?"

"You know exactly what I mean," I pushed. "Why the fuck did you come here? After all the times we could've seen each other, after that stupid game night you'd planned on my late wife's death anniversary so 'I wouldn't be alone', you just push me off with some stupid letters and then show up out of nowhere during one of my highest profile jobs in months, no Idhynth in sight, and for what? To 'help us out'? You said you wanted to tell me something before you just fucked me, so do it. Tell me."

Rosanna's jaw tensed, hands fidgeting at her sides. Her silence was louder than any words she could've mustered. I let out a long breath and accepted what I'd been pushing away for months.

"We appreciate your help, but we'll handle the bardic boys and their diadem without you."

"Rhem, I swear I can explain, if you could just wait—"

"I'm tired of waiting for you."

Hiding the tears welling in my eyes, I turned and left, avoiding sharp stalagmites and slippery rubble as I made my way back to Benny. Morally Gone's performance was about to start, and I couldn't waste anymore time with a woman who couldn't make up her mind. I needed to focus on killing these guys, leaving this shithole of a festival, and getting our coin.

Benny stared at me with his red eyes. *Want to talk about it?*

I took a deep breath, unsheathed my axe, and cracked my neck. *Maybe when we get drunk later. For now, I'd rather kill some idiotic men and steal their diadem.*

Benny nodded. ***Then let's go kick some immortal buns and collect our bounty!***

I turned to him. "Ass up. Face down—"

Can't lose!

6

WHO'S YOUR DADDY?

I WISH I could've said it was a mystery to solve how to open the door to Morally Gone's backstage entrance, a little story where I could explain how Benny and I figured out the puzzle that these shadow-obsessed idiots had devised, but that was the thing—they were idiots.

The bardic boy band who had stolen the Diadem of Ancient Darkness and Devoted Yearning, the ones who were about to use said object to enchant a cavern full of fans into becoming their brainwashed slaves, had decided to erect a statue of themselves as their backstage doorway. Naked, smirking, and striking poses like they were trying to sell non-existent underwear. Their dicks stuck out as long as my arm and were sculpted as thick as my thighs (a significant girth).

"Grab our thick cocks, pull them down, and we'll make sure you never drown," I said, quoting the sign hung above the statue. "Subtle."

Those are lyrics from their latest album! Benny commented. *I never realized how salacious they were.*

"How could you possibly miss that?"

Because I get lost in the music, Rhema. Lyrics are just a vehicle for the beat!

"And this is why idiots like them get away with so much bullshit," I sighed.

Well, if we want to discuss media literacy in music, I published an entire article on it in the Dragon Studies Peer-Reviewed Scholastic Journal last month! You see, community and continent-wide events tend to influence pop culture on a much broader scale than most realize. Corporations that own musical groups like Morally Gone bend and shape songs to gain more profit in light of those aforementioned current events—

"Benny, I can't stress enough how we don't have time for this, so could you pull on their stone cocks so we can get in there and kill them?"

He snorted. *Well, Miss I-don't-stay-informed-on-current-events-like-my-very-smart-and-talented-dragon, I think it might be time for you to face your fear of cocks and do it instead.*

"*What?*" I turned to him. "I'm not afraid of cocks, I just don't like touching the ones with gross veins carved into them."

He raised a scaly brow. *If you're not scared, then prove it.*

"I don't need to prove anything. Just do what I say so we can end this."

You do it.

"You."

YOU.

I took a deep breath. "Alright, neither of us like cocks, I get it. But I *really* don't like them. So, can you just do it? Please?"

Benny tapped a talon on the ground. "Do you promise to read my published article after this?"

I sighed. "Yes, sure, I'll read your article."

All of them?

"All of them? How many have you written?"

Does it matter?

"Yes?"

Then I'm not pulling their cocks.

I groaned. Of all the times for Rosanna to not be around, it would be now. She thinks all genitalia are beautiful and perfect (her words, definitely not mine). A shudder ran down my back as I thought of her broad smile and long, braided hair. She'd fucked me raw just before this, and I'd gotten on my knees like a sinner begging for forgiveness from her queen, and then it was all gone in one breath. I shook the thoughts away. She'd left just like I asked, and there was no reason to start wishing things had ended differently.

It was up to Benny and me to figure this out.

So was I really going to let these nasty sausage-like stone dicks get in the way of retrieving our bounty so we could finally get our coin?

My lack of conviction after asking myself this was, sadly, not a surprise.

"Fine," I said, "I'll read *all* your articles."

Promise?

Promise.

Yippee!

Benny wasted no time wrapping his green and purple talons around each dick and pulling them down. The door opened with a loud scrape.

In most cases, entering through a backstage entrance probably would've been better suited for beings who were not as huge as Benny, not to mention he was still carrying the bloodied, dead musician, Tamii Quick, around his neck.

So, when a conglomerate of Courtchella and Morally Gone assistants dropped their scrolls and steaming mugs of coffee in the backstage cavern hallway, yelling at the top of their lungs, we weren't left with many other routes.

Let's kill these motherfuckers.

Couldn't have said it better myself!

I jumped on his back, ready to soar through the door and

onto the stage, but what I wasn't ready for was the emptiness behind me. Rosanna's hands weren't gripping my waist, her laughter no longer in my ear. But it was better this way. I didn't need Rosanna, I had Benny–familiar, reliable, and my anchor through the toughest storms.

And disgustingly realistic cocks.

Benny surged forward. We soared past orb lights of every color along screaming people and crude drawings of dicks and tits on the wall with Morally Gone's signatures next to them. I fastened my goggles and readied myself for the pungent smell of sweat mixed with musk. If shadow magic was all they had to work with, then Benny and I could take them out in one swoop.

He hummed his theme song as we flew through an alcove, the path shooting us into Morally Gone's performance cavern.

If Courtchella's main entrance could've fit five Bennys, this one could fit at least ten. Stone-carved seats stacked to the top of the cave ceiling, every single one of them filled with fans wearing purple enchanted lights and holding bright-green enchanted sticks with purple runes on their foreheads.

The stage glowed the brightest, the Diadem of Ancient Darkness and Devoted Yearning rune carved into its entirety. With each musical note, the giant rune pulsed, matching the crowd's foreheads.

If we were going to stop this ritual and collect our bounty, we needed to kill Morally Gone and retrieve the diadem.

Let's hit it, I instructed.

Benny swooped around to get a clear shot of the bardic boy band, but before he could, we crashed into a shadowed figure.

Hold on tight!

Benny flipped mid-air. My forearms strained as I fought to keep hold of his reins. Claws facing the cave wall, Benny slammed into it with such force that air rushed out of my chest. My feet slipped out of the stirrups. Ribs aching and eyes blurry, I dangled parallel to the wall, but I refused to let go of the reins.

Instead, I focused on drawing my belly button in as tight as I could, swinging my legs up, and securing my feet back into the stirrups.

What the fuck was that? I asked.

Looks like it's your favorite thick-dick friends.

Turning my head, I saw the cavern ceiling wasn't decorated with just purple and green orb lights, but large dark silhouettes hanging from the ceiling.

How many gross bats can these guys have? I groaned.

At least thirteen, at most thousands!

Not helpful. I sighed. *Alright, if you could just blast them with fire, then we can get on with this.*

No can do, Rhemy boo. If debris starts falling like what happened in the main cavern, I won't be able to fly!

Then I guess it's time for more dinner.

If I eat one more, my tummy will explode.

A memory of years ago played through my mind, Benny eating so much butter he puked nonstop. There was no way in hells I was living through that again.

Great, so we're just going to hang on the side of the cave and watch thousands of people get put under a permanent enchantment while we lose our chance at collecting the bounty?

We certainly could, or—Benny gave me a mischievous grin—**we could do Falling Goat.**

Perfect idea. Throw me at Morally Gone's stage wall and then all the bats can swarm and tackle me with their dicks.

Rhema, come on! You think I'd just let them bully you like that?

You mean kill me.

He ignored my comment. **I'll be your distraction! I'll fling you over there so you can get on stage, then I'll make a big ruckus so the bats come at me instead.**

What a fucking ridiculous plan.

But, time was running out. Purple shadow magic flowed

from the stage and into the crowd as Morally Gone danced in perfect unison, their leader singing into his enchanted stick.

Smell my musky leather jacket
Breathe it in like your last breath
Taste my lusty shadow magic
Take it all in it's depth

THE GIANT RUNE PULSED BRIGHTER.

Breathe it in
Taste it now
You're going, going
Morally gone.

"Fuck it," I said. "Let's do Falling Goat."
YES. Just tell me when and I'll throw you like a football.
A what-ball?
Don't worry about it. Ready?
Unsheathing my axe, I gripped Benny's reins with my other hand and crouched on my saddle. The wall framing the stage looked like it was made of crumbling earth, perfect for my axe to bite into.
Set, I said.
HIKE!
I pushed off Benny right as he whipped his tail. Wind rushed through my hair as I secured my hands on my axe's hilt. Bat screeches sounded behind me. I arced through the air and slammed into the wall, axe buried into the rock, my muscles screaming in protest. Sliding down the rock face, I gritted my teeth and held on until I landed on the side-stage. I yanked my axe out of the wall with a crunch.

So, uh, Rhemy, the bats aren't as distractible as I thought.

WHAT? I spun around.

Sure enough, a bat was about to fly straight into me, its dangling dick flopping in the air.

Face your fear of cocks, Rhemy!

You've got to be kidding me.

I met one of its teeth with my blade, narrowly dodging its flaccid member in the process. My feet slipped against the rubble, the bat pushing me into the wall. I released my blade from its hold. The bat's dick arced in a large circle. Diving onto my shoulder, away from the wall, I narrowly missed its dick slapping my face. Instead, it grazed the split-ends of my hair.

I stilled.

Bat dick touched my hair.

MY HAIR.

Its purple eyes flashed, but I was done running from this. Benny was right: I had to face my fears. I had to cut this cock off once and for all.

It swooped for me. I ran and pushed off the wall, arcing into the air, clearing the bat's attack. The creature crashed into the wall. Debris fell from the ceiling. As it turned around, its floppy cock slinging up and down, I sprung into action. I lifted my heels, shot forward, and swung my weapon down on the bat's girthy, horrifyingly disgusting cock.

Its screech filled the cave with such intensity, Morally Gone missed a choreo beat. The stage's rune flickered.

This was my chance.

I ran for the main stage. Xzander and his boy band members waved at me with wide smiles, the diadem's gem glowing with a bright purple rune on Xzander's head. They didn't stop their performance or even seem to care I was sprinting at them with my axe.

Didn't they realize they were about to die?

I leapt into the air, arcing over Xzander to get the perfect angle to slice his neck. I swung. The crowd gasped. It went clean through like I'd just sliced Benny a large piece of blueberry butter.

I landed on one knee, breaths heavy and arms trembling.

"That was cute," a low voice said from behind.

My stomach dropped. I turned to find Xzander, head still attached to his body, purple smoke curling around his throat. His little boy band members were still dancing and singing as the crowd went wild at Xzander surviving my attack.

"That's impossible," I breathed. "You should be dead."

He pointed to the diadem. "Not if I sold my soul to the darkness."

I groaned. "Are you fucking serious?"

He sold his soul to the DADDY? Benny asked.

"It's how we're able to use the runes," Xzander smirked. "All we had to do was promise the DADDY we'd feed it souls every night, and in return, we receive eternal life."

He pulled up his sleeve. Purple runes decorated his arms like poorly drawn tattoos, the symbols glowing purple and pulsing with the stage rune.

"So let me get this straight," I continued, "this some kind of ritual where the diadem's enchantment will take their souls and turn your fans into the diadem's slaves all so you can live forever?"

Benny's high-pitched ringing sounded as he connected to Xzander's mind.

Ooo! Or maybe this is a ritual where everyone forfeits their soul in hopes they can live ignorant lives devoid of empathy, allowing them to not feel the sting of life's heavy and unbearable moments, but it'll also cost them the elations of wonderful times with family, friends, and their community?

Xzander looked like he was trying to solve a very simple math equation but couldn't remember why one plus one equaled two.

"Uh, yes, hm, the first one, I believe," Xzander confirmed.

I scoffed. "And what happens if you can't get your souls?"

The bard's smile faltered. "Then the DADDY will slowly torture us with shadows for the rest of eternity and—wait, why the fuck am I telling you any of this—?"

I lunged for the diadem. With a laugh, he disappeared in a puff of smoke. He reappeared next to the rest of Morally Gone, their song finishing with a final snare beat.

"And let's welcome to the stage our very own security personnel, the one who caught everyone who fell off our dangerous bridge entrance earlier this evening: Rhema!" Xzander announced to the entire cavern.

If those freaks think they'll survive the night, they're in for a rude awakening.

Rhema, hold on, something doesn't feel right.

No more waiting—we need to destroy that diadem before the enchantment's complete.

Wait, look out—!

The crowd rushed the stage. I stopped in my tracks. They weren't rushing for Morally Gone—they were stampeding towards me.

"It's the security personnel from the bridge!" a woman screamed. "She said we could make out once she got here!"

"She said that to me too!" another yelled.

"Oh my gods," a third yelled, "am I about to have my first orgy? My mother was right about Courtchella after all!"

Benny, I seethed, *remind me to never let you be in charge of choosing the bounty jobs we take after this.*

To be fair, I never said you'd make out with them, he whispered.

I sheathed my axe before any of the people could get skewered. Hot, sweaty bodies mauled me. All of them were either so high or so drunk or so enchanted that they didn't seem to understand who was who. It was impossible to get out of the tangle without hurting them.

Benny, could use some help here!

I'm stuck in a rather exhilarating chase with these bats! They just won't seem to die, and their fangs are A LOT sharper than the ones from the passage.

Shit.

Morally Gone had started their next song—the final one—which meant the enchantment would be complete in three to four minutes according to standardized pop song trends. No matter what I did—throwing elbows, clawing at clothes, or even biting skin—the horny mob wouldn't let me go.

Not only were these Morally Gone losers eternally attached to this damn diadem, but they were about to brainwash thousands of innocents in this cavern, surrendering their autonomy to a group of men who had created statues that required pulling on their dicks.

What had the world come to?

The ground shook. All the wrestling and grabbing for me stopped with it. Morally Gone paused their song.

Are you doing this?

Nope.

Then what's going on? I can't see anything through this mob.

I don't kno— NO WAY.

I took advantage of the mob's surprise, elbowing through them until I could see the cavern again.

The center stage exploded with dirt, Morally Gone's song disrupted and their rune destroyed. They cried out. Xzander disappeared into the shadows. Emerging from the rubble was a large scaly wyrm. On its back sat a woman in an armored halter top, one of her swords drawn.

My heart lurched into my throat.

Rosanna and Gegraz had just destroyed Morally Gone's enchantment.

YOU JUST HAD TO MAKE IT WEIRD

INVIGORATED by Rosanna and Gegraz the wyrm's entrance, I maneuvered out of the disgustingly sweaty dogpile of people. Once I could finally breathe, more desperate hands managed to grab my arms, legs, and ass, dragging me back into what was turning into a gross orgy.

I yelled for Rosanna. She jumped off Gegraz's back and onto the destroyed stage with such confident grace it was like a goddess dismounting her chariot.

"Rhema," she shouted, "did you remember to put on that herbal ointment I gave you?"

I yelled, "What the fuck are you talking about?"

"The ointment for your ass rash!"

Everyone in the dogpile stopped moving.

"What'd you say?" one of them asked Rosanna. "Something about this person we want to have sex with having a rash?"

"Yeah," Rosanna replied, "she got it from fucking a satyr last week. It's horribly contagious. One touch of her sweat and you'll get it too. Can turn your genitals inside out in its most extreme cases. We're pretty sure that's what's happening to her."

The people turned to me, eyes wide with disgust and concern.

Gods, I really needed to stay in more.

"Ow," I yelled, "I think my vagina is dying!"

Everyone screamed, scrambling off me and rushing off the stage, tripping over their pants at their ankles. I wiped off all their sweat and turned to Rosanna. She gave me a thumbs-up.

"The satyr was a nice touch," I huffed.

"Thanks, thought of it on the spot." She smiled. "Now, you and Benny need to go after Morally Gone."

Gegraz's low-pitched ringing sang in my ears. *The very persuasive and surprisingly violent human and I will kill the fat dick creatures, Benny. Take your rider and kill the stupid shadow boy with the tiara.*

Gegraz rushed forward and ate three bats in one gulp. Rosanna leapt on the wyrm's tail, running up until she was able to jump and grab a bat in her throat-slitting chokehold.

Gods, what an idiot I'd been this entire night. Pushing her away, pretending I felt nothing but resentment, toying with the idea of never seeing her after this.

The truth was clear: I wanted Rosanna.

But that revelation had to wait, because I had a job to finish.

Xzander, Morally Gone's leader, reappeared in the audience. Purple smoke trailed behind him as he rushed up the cavern stairs towards the exit, leaving his boy band members on stage to cry and wet themselves.

Benny's gold scales glinted against the orb lights as he swooped down, the dead musician still hanging around his neck like some misogynistic martyr. I grabbed Benny's reins, swung onto my saddle, and pushed my boots into the stirrups.

Follow the purple smoke, I instructed. *We're going to do your favorite move.*

BUTTER SLICE?

Butter slice.

Like a knife cuts through butter
Or a sword cuts through butter
Or an axe cuts through butter
These creeps will soon know
Their heads are like butter
They slice clean like butter
And taste great with butter
Butter slice head to toe.

Xzander scrambled towards an emergency exit, not bothering to look back as he climbed over people who wanted his autograph, his clothes, and even to carry his babies.

"Out of the way, you filthy repulsive people!" Xzander screamed.

Now, Benny.

He dove, flying as low as he could get without his painted talons ripping into people's flesh. The Diadem of Ancient Darkness & Devoted Yearning glinted in the dispersing purple smoke. Hands tightening on my axe, I arched my weapon over my head, biting my tongue until blood trickled in my mouth.

Then, I jumped.

Come on, Rhema, you need to say it!

I'm not going to say it!

But it's too perfect to pass up.

I don't care.

Please? For me?

I sighed, wind whipping through my clothes. If it was for Benny's sake, then I guess I'd better fucking say the damn thing.

The diadem glinted one last time before my axe met its purple gem—right where it was most vulnerable. Xzander's face was priceless: double chin, a twitchy eye, and drool hanging from his mouth

The diadem cracked in half.

"Xzander," I yelled, "who's your DADDY?"

He screamed the same way a man who says "well, actually" might if a woman just told him to stop mansplaining. Unfathomable pressure erupted from the gem, the force traveling through my axe, into my arms, until it hit my chest. I flew backwards. Warm hands caught me. A full set of familiar tits pushed into my back.

Xzander and Morally Gone vanished into purple smoke. The glowing forehead runes on every Courtchella attendee vanished with them. I let out a long, deep breath.

We'd completed the job.

"Nice work out there," Rosanna said.

"I hope that was sarcasm," I replied, releasing myself from her hold. "You and Gegraz had impeccable timing."

She sheathed her swords. "I ran into him on my way out, and once he asked me where the rest of the bats had ended up, I figured you and Benny were in for a nasty surprise."

"Nasty is putting it nicely."

Her smile waned, a small silence sitting between us while Gegraz ate more bats and Benny cheered him on with a theme song that sounded like it was from their spelunking days.

Rosanna rubbed the back of her neck. "I'm sorry for everything, Rhema. What I said, what I've done—"

I held up my hand. She stopped talking.

"You might think I'm about to give you a profound, self-actualized speech about my feelings towards you," I said, stomach cramping, "but I'm probably going to puke out my guts if we don't get out of this disgusting cave as soon as possible."

Rosanna's face contorted from concern to a smile. "Then let's get out of this festival shithole."

Gegraz led the three of us through the backstage door we had entered through, leading us out of the Courtchella caves and into the brisk night air with a path he had made. Before we parted ways, Gegraz made a very serious oath on Benny's green and purple talons, promising he would begin a diet of rabbits and various forms of lettuce to promote his gut health.

"Benny, why don't you give Tamii to Gegraz?" I suggested, the dead musician still hanging from Benny's neck.

He's full of poisonous darts, Rhema!

"Exactly, let him take care of it."

Benny's eyes dilated. *But Rhemy, I didn't even get Morally Gone's signature, and I really want a souvenir.*

I sighed. Rosanna chuckled. Gegraz shrugged.

You promised!

"Did I?"

Benny dilated his eyes further, tears glistening within.

"Fine. But you're getting rid of him tomorrow."

Deal!

Finally, after what felt like days but was only a handful of hours, we left Courtchella: Beneath the Bluffs.

Stars burned in the sky, the fresh air like a splash of cold water in my face, perfect after being stuck in a sweaty, musky— yes, *musky*—cave for four hours too long. Rosanna's hands were wrapped loosely around my stomach, no pinky finger grazing my belly button or breaths brushing along my ear.

Was it pathetic I kind of missed it?

The heart wants what the heart wants, Rhemy boo, Benny crooned into my mind. *Even if the mind knows that's not what's good for it.*

I sighed. *I'm going to tell her, Benny.*

Wait WHAT? You're going to tell her you have feelings for her? That's the plan.

Oh yes, my sweet wonderful frightening and grumpy Rhemy, you're going to be so amazing at sharing your deep, deep secrets! Is there anything you need from me? I can grab a bouquet of flowers? Some heart-shaped chocolates? A cute little "Will-You-Be-My-Strong-Muscle-Mommy-Cupid" card—?

What I'll need from you is silence.

Yes, silence, alright. I can do that! he grinned, Tamii still hanging from his throat like a rag doll missing half its face.

An inn with warm lights glowed beneath us. Rosanna volunteered to pay for food and lodging as an apology for taking us through a passageway with big-dicked bats. Considering all we'd been through, I didn't argue with her offer.

We landed with a light thud, dust swirling at our feet as Rosanna and I dismounted Benny. He requested a big bowl of stew and the thickest slice of butter they could offer. Knowing Rosanna, she'd ask for them to give him two, which she did. We ate our stews, revelling in the warmth during a particularly chilled night for being this close to spring. After, Benny left to collect our bounty at the nearby guild, leaving Rosanna and I to grab a few ales in the inn's tavern.

Warm torchlight flickered over Rosanna's face, her full lips and dark eyes glittering in the soft glow. Her fingers tapped against the wood table, eyes looking anywhere but at me. Grabbing my first of three ales, I downed it in a few gulps.

If there was any time to tell her I finally knew what I wanted —*who* I wanted—it would be now.

I slammed my pint down, the glass mug slipping from my fingers. It shot across the tabletop, my attempts to grab it only sending it further and faster until it sailed over the table's lip and shattered on the ground.

I cursed. Rosanna tried *very* hard not to laugh. The barkeep came over in a fuss, shooing me away as they cleaned the mess with a few sweeps and a small enchantment. As they left our table, they murmured about how their day had kept getting worse after hearing Morally Gone was brutally devoured by a couple of Courtchella bats.

Rosanna and I hid our smiles.

"So," I started, heart beating so fast it hurt, "I've been thinking—"

"Before you say anything, Rhem, Idyhnth just finished her spa time and is on her way," she interrupted. "I've got to get back to the fae realm soon."

Who knew excitement could turn into dread faster than Benny could eat butter.

"Oh, right, of course," I said, taking a swift drink.

We stared at our ales for an excruciatingly long time. Still, I needed to share what was burning in my chest—

"Rhem, we can't keep doing this," Rosanna finally said, "you were right earlier today. I've made you wait longer than you deserve."

I cursed myself. "I was upset."

"And you were right to be upset. I didn't show on an important night–one of many. I'd promised to support you, and I couldn't be there. You deserve someone who can follow through on their word."

As I rubbed the back of my neck with one hand, I drank my ale with the other. "And that can't be you?"

Rosanna stared at me with distant eyes.

"Rhem," she said softly, "I'm out there in the fae realm chasing bounty after bounty, and that's what I do. That's where I have to be. Where I *want* to be."

That last line. I tried not to let it sink past my skin and into my chest, but it did. It always fucking did with her.

"Then you should be there," I whispered.

"I know," she replied, "and you should be here, with Benny, killing those godsawful men and saving the women and people they prey on. You're good at it—brilliant, actually."

Crossing my arms, I looked at the ceiling, forcing the tears to stay behind my eyes.

"I'm sorry for everything," Rosanna continued. "I'm sorry for abandoning you the night of your late wife's death anniversary and the times before that, too. And I'm sorry for showing up to your job unannounced and for making it twenty times harder than it needed to be." She paused, tapping her fingers on her pint glass. "Trust me when I say I wish I'd been there every time."

I gulped, asking slowly, "Why weren't you?"

She stilled her hand on her pint. Her breaths quickened, gaze looking to the ceiling, her hands, the table—anywhere but me.

"I—"she shuddered, "Rhem, it's just, I can't—"

Sweat dripped down her forehead, a deep red burning along her cheeks. For as long as I'd known her, Rosanna had always known what to say. So it was strange, in this moment, to witness her grasping for words like smoke. And if she didn't want to tell me—*couldn't*—then I'd let it be. I'd never force her to share anything she wasn't ready to offer.

No matter how much I wanted her to.

"I'm glad you came," I interrupted.

She paused and looked into my eyes.

"I'll admit, I hated it at first," I confessed. "I was upset with you, didn't want to talk to you ever again, tried to ignore you. But the reality is that I missed you, Rosanna, so even though this Courtchella mess turned into a shitshow, I'm glad you came." I paused. "And I forgive you."

Tears glistened in her eyes. She tilted her head back and finished her ale.

"Thank you, Rhem."

I finished mine, too. "So what now?"

She folded her hands. "I think we should remain friends."

"As opposed to...?"

"As opposed to whatever we've been doing."

"Fucking?" I suggested.

She chuckled. "Yes, fucking, and the letters..."

The sadness was so unbearable, I laughed instead. I guess that's how I usually handled shit like this—why cry when it could be hilarious?

"It's honestly annoying," I finally said, "how we fuck one time two years ago and then a part of me expected we'd just be in each other's lives."

She straightened. "What do you mean?"

"You were probably one of the best fucks of my life *and* you're actually a good time to be around, so I wanted to see you more." I shrugged. "Also, don't tell my late wife I said that. No need to make her jealous in her afterlife."

Rosanna coughed up some of her second ale. I laughed. Not easy to catch her off guard, and I had to admit, I was proud of that one.

"My lips are sealed," she managed to get out, wiping spit off her mouth. "And you're not a bad fuck yourself. You can even be a decent time, too."

"Wow. *Decent.*"

Rosanna smirked, and I couldn't stop the smile peeling across my lips.

"If we're going to be just friends, you better stop wearing that halter top whenever I see you," I said with a sly smile.

She laughed. "Really does it for you, hm? Is it the side boob?"

"Side boob, under boob, front boob—any boob, really."

"Then you better work on covering that face scar of yours," she winked.

I raised a brow. "Really? Wow, learn something new every day."

"I've said it before."

"If it was during sex then I definitely wasn't paying attention to anything but that damn sword dildo of yours."

She pushed her tongue between her teeth and laughed

again. I fucking loved that sound: warm, bright, exciting. If I could find a way to make her laugh every second, I would.

The heaviness suspended in the air lifted. She was being honest, the exact part of her I'd been wanting more than anything these past couple of months. I just didn't realize how much it was going to fucking hurt.

"Idhynth's here," she sighed, "so I'll see you sometime soon? You did make a promise to paint her talons."

My chest deflated. "If not the next guild celebration, maybe the Butter & Barmaids Festival in the spring. I'll bring a blue color to match her scales."

"She'll love that." Rosanna extended her hand. "I'll see you there, *friend*."

I looked at her hand, then her face. "You just had to make it weird, didn't you?"

"Weird? It's just a handshake, for gods sake."

"You fucked me no less than two hours ago, and you want me to shake your hand and say 'friends'? Come on, Rosanna."

Putting her hands up, she admitted defeat. "Alright, alright. It was weird."

"Thank you."

She stood up, lingering at the side of the table for a few moments. I couldn't stop that spark from lighting in my chest, hoping she would change her mind.

"Goodbye, Rhema."

I offered my goodbye, and she left without another word. I wasn't sure how long I sat at the table, squeezing my head between my hands, before Benny's unmistakable talon knocked at my mental wall. It fell with barely a whisper.

Rhema, you won't BELIEVE what just happened—wait, how did it go? Are you two madly in love now?!

I finished my third and final ale. *Everything's great, Benny. Perfect. Amazing. I'm pregnant and we're getting married tomorrow.*

So things went to shit?

"Shit" is putting it nicely.

That bad? Yikes.

Didn't you see her and Idhynth before they left?

Idhynth came by? Well, I must've missed her, Benny replied.

How? She's huge.

Rhema! Don't ever use that word to describe a dragon again! The correct term us dragons prefer is MASSIVE.

Alright. She's massive.

That's better. And no, I didn't see them leave otherwise I would've sung them a lovely tune.

I sighed. *Makes no damn sense, but alright.*

Did you at least speak from the heart?

I tried.

Benny hummed a soft melody. **Then you did great, Rhemy.**

We sat in comfortable silence until Benny's voice escalated close to a shriek.

Now back to my news: we fucked up the bounty!

What are you talking about?

Alright, so, turns out the bounty was for killing Morally Gone AND retrieving the diadem, which you forgot—

WE forgot—

—which you forgot to pick up after killing Xzander, so we got less than half of the promised coin. So sad!

I leaned back and grunted at the ceiling. *Could this night get any worse?*

Well here's the thing, Rhema—we actually got even MORE coin from a different bounty: Tamii Quick!

WHAT?

YES! It turned out there WAS a bounty on his head. I guess Tamii's ex-mate loves to dine at this tavern with her new Star Flame Court lover, and when I sang a goodnight song to them on their way out—which I've been doing for everyone out of joyous courtesy when I returned—she recognized Tamii's tattered clothes and showed me the bounty poster she'd JUST made after he

released his new single tonight. She even gave us extra coin for returning him to her in such a mangled state! Benny squealed.

Are you serious?

We've got enough coin to last us several months, Rhem!

SEVERAL MONTHS?

I sprinted out of the tavern and ran out to Benny. Sure enough, he'd been guarding a stockpile of gold with his tail, reciting some dumb lines from a play he once saw about a dragon hoarding gold. I didn't bother to tell him that's what most people thought of dragons nowadays.

Rhema, we just saved thousands of people from being turned into mindless minions by one of the most notorious, nasty, misogynistic bardic boy bands in history. WE NEED TO CELEBRATE!

He slapped me with his tail, and I smiled at the glee sparkling in his eyes. The weight from my conversation with Rosanna dissipated into the night air, replaced with something else—something lighter. As I looked at Benny, I knew what Rosanna had said was right: Benny and I belonged here, doing what we did best.

You're right, Benny. We do deserve to celebrate. I patted his scales. *I mean, I don't think I've ever seen us pull off Falling Goat and Butter Slice with that much finesse.*

That's what I've been trying to tell you! Benny exclaimed. *Ok, here's my order for the night: I'll take three sticks of butter, two with garlic and one with dill, and then I'll have the...*

After I ordered Benny's horde of butter and my endless supply of ale, we sat by the bonfire until the stars disappeared into the morning light. We recounted our worst and best moments of Courtchella, from bridge duty to Tamii Quick, from Gegraz all the way to destroying the diadem. And, I might've been convinced by Benny to learn another piece of choreography from the now-dead bardic boy band, Morally Gone.

What? After all's said and done, they *did* make decent music.

THE EN—

*RHEMA, **are we going to tell them about our next adventure? You KNOW the people love it when we give them a little teaser!***

Benny, they just finished the story and I'm still recovering from it too. Maybe next time.

RHEMA I WANT TO SHARE ABOUT OUR NEXT ADVENTURE.

Good gods, alright, fine, if it'll stop you shouting so loud in my head then go right ahead.

Great, thank you. Ahem, where was I? Oh YES. We're so excited to announce that at least one if not several thousand more of our adventures—

A.J. told us two, Benny—

Will be coming out this year! So stay tuned, especially if you're still wondering what in the hibbly jibbly Rosanna's been up to.

Can we not talk about her right now? I'm moving on to greener pastures.

Of course you are, Rhemy.

I don't appreciate the sarcasm.

No sarcasm here. Never ever.

Alright, that's it, we're done here.

WAIT, but what about telling them about CostCourt and all the shit that's about to happen—?

Goodbye and goodnight, we'll see you all on our next adventure.

ACKNOWLEDGMENTS

I'm so excited to have Benny & Rhema's second adventure in the books! It's no mystery that this past summer's obsession with KPop Demon Hunters deeply inspired a boy band-themed bounty hunter quest, and who best to do it with than our grumpy muscle mommy and our sunshine dragon?

First off, I want to give a HUGE thank you and shout out to my spouse, PJ, who is the genius behind all of Benny's and Morally Gone's songs in this story! He's a lyrical genius who whips them up in less than 5 minutes. So, if you find yourself praising me for those songs, make sure to find him at @portableworlds on IG and shower him in the devotion he deserves. However, I will take some credit for Tamii Quick's song—my pride and joy.

Second, I want to give a big shout out to my Bardsy writing group: Adam Simon, C.C. Tyler, Justin, and Kimberly Straub. There's no better people I can think of to throw my most insane ideas at to help me establish Benny & Rhema's crazy, satirical little world alongside its heartfelt core. You all aren't afraid to let me know when something's amiss and offer some of the most profound insight to help me push through the initial first and second draft phases. Thank you for helping me breathe life into this story!

Third, I want to thank my beta readers: Alex Bree, N.C. Scrimgeour, K.C. Woodruff, P.C. Nottingham, and Sofia B.— each of you are so skilled in your writing and storytelling craft to which my stories always benefit! And my other group of beta readers: Sofia, M.X. Burns, Alex, and Grace K.—thank you for your absolutely unhinged comments and helpful pointers to make sure this story was as cohesive and strong as possible.

Fourth: my lovely and amazing PA, Grace Keheley (@barbies.bookloft)! Where would this book be without you? Probably still swimming around in my brain waiting to be written. If it wasn't for your unending support, hype, and help as I got myself up off the ground and back into my writing routine, then we wouldn't have our second Benny & Rhema story until who knows when. Thank you for enduring my phone call rants and unendingly unhinged voice memos. It was such a fun and enlightening season working with you and I wouldn't have traded it for the world.

Fifth: my incredible editor, Ashley (Aspen Editorial). You never cease to go above and beyond to make sure my stories are as smooth as possible for my readers. I always let out a breath I didn't know I was holding whenever I get your edits back, because I know it's finally legible. My endless gratitude to you, always!

And lastly, thank you to my readers. Without you, Benny & Rhema would just be a tree falling in the forest with no one to hear their ridiculous banter and whimsical songs. And with that, make sure you go out and do something whimsical today —the world needs more of it and especially needs more of you!

More adventures to come your way SOON.